A MOTHER'S TALE

& OTHER STORIES

KHANH HA

C&R Press
Conscious & Responsible

C&R Press
Conscious & Responsible
crpress.org

For special discounted bulk purchases, please contact:
C&R Press sales@crpress.org
Contact info@crpress.org to book events, readings and author signings.

A MOTHER'S TALE

For Judith Shepard

Grateful acknowledgment is made to the following publications, in which the stories of this collection originally appeared: *Heartbreak Grass* (Greensboro Review); *A Bridge Behind* (Eastlit Journal); *In a Far Country* (Waccamaw Journal); *The River of White Water Lilies* (Moon City Review); *The American Prisoner* (Permafrost Magazine); *The Virgin's Mole* (Verdad); *A Mother's Tale* (Louisiana Literature); *The Leper Colony* (Thrice Fiction); *The Red Fox* (Zymbol); *The General Is Sleeping* (Red Earth Review); *All the Pretty Little Horses* (The Museum of Americana).

Contents

Heartbreak Grass

There was a man who lived in my district and this man had gone South to fight the Americans and when he came back a year and a half later he had no arms, no legs, and he was blind.

I called him Uncle, like us youngsters would address their seniors. Uncle Chung was thirty-one when he returned home as a quadruple amputee. A blind war veteran. I was eighteen and about to be drafted to join those destined for the South. When I saw Uncle Chung the first time, I knew why many boys my age grew alarmed of being drafted into the army. Uncle Chung used to work as a machinist. He was once a big man. But the first time I saw him, now limbless, he looked to me more like a freak I saw years later in the South, a country boy burned by napalm so far gone he looked during nighttime like a glowworm and his father would charge each neighborhood kid ten xu to come into the house to watch the human mutant.

I saw Uncle Chung on a day Huan's father, the herbalist, sent me over to the man's house with the medicine. The medicine. Always the medicine. And the wife. Each time Uncle Chung's wife came to the shop to consult with the herbalist, I would hang back, so I could listen to her melodious voice and steal glances at her while trying to look busy in the shop. She was in her mid-twenties, but she looked older, the way she rolled her hair up and tucked it into a bun, so when she turned her head you could see the long nape of her neck. She always wore a white or pale blue blouse. Just white or pale blue. And always the first customer when the shop opened. The early morning light would cast a pallor on her face, and her ink-black eyebrows only made her face seem paler. Yet despite the white of the undernourished, the unwell look, she was beautiful. The city was full of women her age and older. Now and then you saw men— many had gone South and most of them never returned.

One rainy morning I went to their house with the medicine. Down an alley through the standing water with floating trash, to a stucco-yellow matchbox dwelling in a housing project. Its green door was left ajar. Stepping in, I heard a man singing:

> *If I were a dove*
> *I'd be a snow-white dove.*

Spring and then summer.
The flowers, the flowers, the flowers.
You say aren't they pretty
And I say
Aren't they really.

I looked down at the man sitting on the pallet. The gruff voice stopped, the man turned his face toward the door. His skin, his eyeballs were yellow, the mucus yellow. I couldn't tell if he was blind, but his eyes had the look of fake eyes you put in stuffed animals. His song about the pretty flowers struck me. What could he see now but his own memories? He kept nodding—I wasn't sure if he had any control of it—and he had a large head matted with tousled black hair that covered his ears and the collar of his shirt. The old olive-colored army shirt, with its long sleeves cut off, revealed the stumpy ends of his severed arms. You could see the rotten-wood brown of the flesh—what was left of his upper arms.

I told him I brought him the medicine and as I spoke I looked at his full wiry beard. If his wife refused to shave it for him, I thought, it would one day hang down past his neck. He must have been a big man; aside from his large head, the only part left of him, his torso, filled out his army shirt. His chest was as thick as a boar. He wiggled on his rump. "Make me a pipe," he said as if he knew me, or I were someone he used to boss around.

I stood eyeing him, a squat hunk of meat sitting on two slabs of flesh. What looked like his shorts were a pair of army trousers shorn at the knees.

"Don't stand there!" he snapped at me, his voice viscous, as if spoken through a mouthful of glutinous rice.

"I brought your medicine, Uncle," I said and bent to put the herb packet next to a water pipe that sat before him. It was a long bamboo pipe. Near the bowl the yellow had become stained with black smoke. The pipe stood on an angle, harnessed by a wide bamboo strip that went around the pipe's trunk and came down to rest on the ground like a mortar tube on its bipod.

"Make the pipe," he said. "Then you can go."

I just shook my head.

"Don't you know how to light a pipe? Boy?"

"I do, Uncle."

"Then light my damned pipe. And get out!"

Light your own pipe! But I stopped short of ridiculing him. I didn't pity him. At first sight, he struck me as freakish. An overbearing freak. Then I thought I'd better set the tone for myself.

"You'll see a lot of me, Uncle," I said to him politely, "as long as you need Chinese medicine. And I don't take orders. Not from strangers."

"You a prince?" His voice twanged. "Some sort of a pampered shit?"

"If I were, Uncle, I wouldn't be here bringing you this medicine."

"Did your Pa teach you manners? Or is he too busy making drugs?"

"My Ma and Pa died a long time ago."

"So you're an orphan. No wonder."

"I can behave, Uncle."

My calm voice had him lost for a moment. He rotated his jaw, then asked, "How old are you?"

"Eighteen, Uncle."

"You be joining the army soon, eh?"

"Right. The way things are."

"You know what I did for a living before the war?"

"What did you do, Uncle?"

"I was a foreman in a machine shop."

I pictured lathes and mills. Those shops must be busy during wartime. Hearing nothing from me, he leaned his head to one side as if to determine where I was. "In the army I was a senior sergeant," he said. That fit him, I thought. Some were domineering by nature. He went on, "Used to do all the things myself. My woman didn't need to lift a finger. Now, now, the world's turned upside down. Man has to beg from a woman's hand. When you're down and out, you're worse than a mutt. I can't even piss or shit unless she lets me."

His voice was flat, but I sensed no self-pity. Like he was telling me about the weather. I thought of walking out, but I changed my mind. I could see the pipe's bowl had no tobacco. "Where's your set, Uncle?" I asked.

"Look around," he said tonelessly. "Set's shaped like a persimmon."

The bare room had two metal chairs. Under one chair sat a lidded pot. It looked like his toilet pot. The only piece of furniture was a black-wood cupboard. The ornate flowers embossed on the cupboard's doors gave it a vintage feel. It must have belonged to his once-proud past, before the war ruined him.

"Can't find it?" he asked, keeping his head still as if to listen for a sign of my presence. "Used to have things everywhere around here. But she's sold most of them. Now you can hear the echo of your voice."

Through a thin flowered curtain that sectioned off the interior of the house, I saw a bamboo cot draped with a mosquito net. The net hadn't been rolled up. I went through the curtain looking around. A gas stove sat against the yellow-painted wall next to a stand-alone narrow cabinet, its black-wood glass doors opaque with smoke and dust. On the wall were hung rattan baskets dyed plum red and peach yellow. A wooden table sat in the center of the room, and on the table I saw the persimmon-shaped caddy painted coal black. The caddy made of fruitwood had a keyhole. I brought it to him. It was locked. I told him.

"Damn woman," he said.

"She keeps the key?"

"Damn, she did."

"She forgot?"

"That woman? Never. Never forgets anything."

"Well, Uncle," I chuckled. "What's with the key anyway? Even if she left it for you, I mean."

"I've got help." He jerked his chin toward the entrance. "Door's always open."

"Your neighbors?"

"Them louts. Sit at the door every day. Gawking and giggling."

"Ah, kids. They help you, Uncle?"

"Some do. Some I have to bribe."

I wondered what he bribed them with. "Where is she now?"

"Out. Business."

I shook the herb packet for him to hear. "What's this medicine for, Uncle?"

"Stabilize the *yin* and *yang* in my body. That's what your Pa, eh, the herbalist said."

"Your *yin* and *yang*?"

"This body," he said, pressing his chin to his chest to make a point, "still has a piece of shrapnel in a lung. The metal junk messes up the balance of *yin* and *yang*. So I heard."

"How's that?"

"I puke blood whenever it gets bone chilly."

"They didn't take it out of your lung?"

"If they could, it wouldn't be in my lung now, eh?"

I ignored his remark and looked around. The slatted side door opened into a common garden. I knelt on one knee, looked at the water pipe, then at him. "You smoke often, Uncle?"

"Often as she lets me." He grinned, then yawned.

I could smell his rancid breath. I tapped the caddy until he cocked his head to listen to the noise. "I can make a pipe for you, Uncle," I said. "But I'd have to pry the lock open."

"I don't give a damn about the lock. But I know what she'll do if the lock is busted."

"What then?"

He nodded again, like he was following his thoughts. "Once I lay here in my piss and shit the whole damn day till she decided to clean me up. Otherwise the house would stink and that'd ruin her dinner."

"What started it?"

"Like I told you. I only piss or shit when she lets me."

"So she wanted to condition you, didn't she?"

"You're wrong, boy." He frowned. "I mean, young man, she was talking business with this man in the alley. Talk. Talk. I yelled to her. Damn did I yell. Then everything burst out of me. When she came back in I doubt she bothered to look at me. Then when the smell couldn't be ignored for heaven's sake, she just left the house."

Listening, I recalled her, that beautiful woman, and couldn't reconcile what I just heard with what I'd carried inside me ever since I first saw her. He wiggled on his rump and the nylon sheet that covered the pallet squished. "If I can have me a drink," he said. "Hell, if I can have me some rice liquor."

"Where does she keep it, Uncle?"

"That woman won't waste money on that kind of stuff." He wrinkled his nose, snorting a few times to clear it. "We'd been drinking, me and some old friends. They brought a bottle with them and after they left I began having chills and shaking like a dog. She came in and saw the mess of cigarette butts and ashes and unwashed cups and started yelling at me. I cursed her, so she sat me up and screamed in my face, and it was then I threw up. I believe I just let it gush out all over her blouse."

"You vomited on her? Why?"

"To spite her? I'm not sure. She emptied the bottle into the drain. That's far worse than hearing her curse me or let me rot on my own."

"I'll get you some liquor the next time, Uncle."

"I have no money. To pay you."

"I know."

"I'd appreciate it, young man. You drink?"

"A little."

"That won't hurt. You're going into the army soon. I used to get high while we stayed for months in the jungles. Ever heard of dog roses?"

"They told me. Wild roses that crave blood to bloom?"

"Hogwash." He blew his nose with a loud snort. "But the wild roses have a subdued fragrance, not as strong as garden roses. And their leaves when crushed have a delicious smell. We cut up their fruits too and add them to the tobacco. The rose hips give an added authentic kick when you're high."

His mouth hung open with an amused smile as he stared into space. Those eyes made me think of yellow marbles. Quietly I looked at his limbless torso, the wiry beard that covered half of his face, and a thought hit me: How would I carry on if I became like him? This man seemed to survive the way a creeper did, by latching on to living things nearby. He wanted to live.

*

I went back to Uncle Chung's house a few days later. This time the herb packet I brought contained finely cut leaves of yellow false jasmine. When Huan's father wrapped them up, I asked him what they were for. "For hemorrhoids," he said. "For external swelling and pain. But never take them orally," he said. "It's fatal." I asked if the wife knew about it and he nodded. "She didn't want the ointment," he said. "She wanted the leaves and the seed pods." Much later when I was fighting in the South, I would occasionally come upon this vine in the jungles. At first glance you could mistake it for honeysuckle. Then I found out that the vine—any part of it from its root to its leaves and flowers and fruits—was also toxic if taken by the mouth. I also learned the words the Americans called it: heartbreak grass.

I bought a half liter of rice liquor in a bottle. Uncle Chung was lying on the pallet, sleeping on his side like a big baby. I woke him and helped him sit up. He kept squirming.

"Hemorrhoids bothering you, Uncle?" I asked him.

"Like hangnails," he said. "Just a nuisance. You said you've got the spirits?"

"I bought half a liter."

"Let me smell it."

I opened the bottle and held it under his nose. He leaned forward to have a full whiff of it and nearly toppled. I held him up. He grunted, his face contorted into a painful scowl. The hemorrhoid must be bad enough, I thought.

"You want to lie down, Uncle?"

"What for? Wish I had arms to hug this bottle here. Eh?"

I found a cup and poured him some of the clear-colored spirit and brought the rim of the cup to his lips. He sniffed, then inhaled deeply, his nostrils flaring. Then he thrust his head toward the cup, and said, "Give me." He made a loud sucking sound, lifting his chin in a great effort to imbibe the liquor.

"A smoke, Uncle?"

"Got no key to that caddy." He burped. "You know that."

"I got you cigarettes. Here."

As I lit and puffed on a cigarette for him, he sniffed like a mouse. "You're a prince, young man," he said, and his lips curled up into a wide grin. "If I die tonight, I won't regret a damn bit."

I plugged the cigarette between his lips and let him drag on it. When the ash curled and broke, I caught it in my palm and went to the door and let the rain wash it from my hand.

"We need some sun." I sat back down. "To air things out."

"Rainy day like this, you just want to sit and sip liquor and cuddle up with a pipe. Eh?" He tilted his torso to one side and I could tell that he wanted to ease the pressure on his hemorrhoids.

"This stuff for your hemorrhoids," I said as I jiggled the herb packet, "has it helped?"

"What?" His dead-fish eyes looked blindly at me.

I gave him another shot of rice liquor. Then huffing he said, "Opium might help."

"Opium? You can't afford it, Uncle."

"My woman gets it at the border."

I lit another cigarette and put it between his lips. "You said it helps? Against pain?"

"Kills pain. When I was all busted up by a *mìn cóc*, they gave me opium. Damn. It worked."

"What's a *mìn cóc*?"

He described it. Leaping Frog mine. Gruesome destruction. The kind of mine that jumps up when triggered and explodes two, three feet above the ground. Severs your legs and, worst of all, maims your genitals. Bouncing Betty. That was the name I later learned from the Americans. I asked him if he lost his limbs from a Bouncing Betty, and he said yes, nodding and snorting. He asked me, "Which would you rather lose: both of your legs or your penis?" I said I would never ask myself such a question, for it was a warped sense of humor that should have no place in a sane mind. He chewed on the cigarette butt leisurely and said, "Soon you'll ask yourself such when you start having fears of losing body parts." I told him I never treated one part of my body more favorably than another. If it happened, I'd live with it. One older guy in the army said the same thing to me, years later when I was in the South, that your body parts are like your children and you don't favor one over another. Now, out of curiosity, I asked if he still had his penis and he laughed, spitting out the cigarette, and the ash scattered on the nylon sheet. I brushed off the ash and waited until he stopped cackling and put the cigarette back between his lips. He shook his head, so I took the cigarette out and he said, chortling, "Still with me, young man. My treasure. So I don't have to pee through a tube. And am still a man. Don't ask me about my woman though. I don't blame her." I mused on his remark as he asked for another sip. Afterward he said there was this thing called "crotch cup," which had gained popularity in the South among men in his unit and others. It started out when this guy custom-made a triangle cup-shaped piece that he cut out of an artillery shell, and through its three sides, he drilled holes to run three twines and looped them around his torso to hold the piece in place against his crotch. He became the butt of every joke told among fellow soldiers. Then when more and more men fell victim to Bouncing Betty mines, many having been cut below the waist, their genitals pulverized, blown and stuck to their faces in pieces of skin and hair, they grew so paranoid they started finding ways to protect their manhood—and their lineage. The crotch cup became their holy answer. I tried to absorb the horror of the war, twinged with the knowledge that I, too, would soon be a part of that reality. Then, snickering, he said some fellows in his unit at one point decided to take a break from wearing the crotch cups, and the next thing, they hit Bouncing Betty mines. What he never could forget were the crotch pieces of the army trousers all shredded and glued to fragments of white bones, unrecognizable lumps of the genitals found on the ground, some still with skin, some with hair. Without sight now, he said, he imagined those scenes day and night. I listened and decided to take a sip of liquor. I wasn't afraid, but the gloomy picture he painted affected my mood.

*

I hadn't visited Uncle Chung for more than a month and I hadn't seen his wife coming to the herbal store for prescriptions. One late morning when the weather cleared up, I went to his house. The door was closed but not locked. Inside the house, dim and cool, there was a moistness in the air. It was tinged with a fermented sourness of liquor that had been spilled. On the pallet scattered with clumps of cooked rice, Uncle Chung was lying facedown, the seat of his cutoffs damp-looking. Just as I sat down on my heels, his voice came up, "That you, young man?"

"You awake, Uncle?"

"No. I never sleep," he said with a deep-throated chuckle. "Just airing out my rump."

"Wet your shorts?" I peered through the curtain. "Where is she?"

"Be back in the afternoon. She closed the door, didn't she? Should have left it open for fresh air."

"It smells in here, Uncle. Want me to open it?"

"Well, don't chance it. She closed it for a reason."

"What?"

"Bunch of those kids were coming here this morning. Some were new, I could tell. So she yelled at them, 'You want to peep at him? Do you? How about pay him? That's right. Pay him and I'll let you ogle at him, pet him. Long as you like.' They just broke off and ran."

I eyed the stain on his buttocks. "She meant it, didn't she?"

"It came out of her mouth. So."

I thought of her. The pretty face. The pleasant voice. "Want to sit up, Uncle?"

He twisted his head toward my side. "My back. Can you scratch it?"

I pushed up his army shirt, paused, and brushed off pellets of rice stuck to his back. A warm, sweaty smell rose from his body, and for one brief moment I stared at his back, its bare flesh speckled with black moles like someone had sprinkled raisins on it. His voice drifted sleepily, "She kept telling me . . . those black moles I was born with were flies . . . flies . . . crushed into my skin."

As I scratched him, he squirmed. His stomach groaned. I wondered if he had eaten since the night before. "Get a towel in there . . ." he said. "Check the kettle. Might have some hot water in it. That'll take the itch away."

I found a dish towel hung between the rattan baskets. I reheated the water in the kettle and wet the towel and wrung it as steam wafted up. I saw a bowl with some cooked rice left in it, sitting on the table. A few cubes of fermented tofu lay on top of the rice. Next to the bowl was a glass with some water. But it wasn't water when I sniffed it. Liquor. I took the bowl and the glass with me and came back out. The hot towel seemed to help him feel better against the itch. I scrubbed his back until it turned raw red.

"That damn monkey meat," he slurred.

"What monkey meat?"

"She brought back some monkey meat yesterday. I ate some."

He tried to turn onto his back. With my help he rolled over. His left cheek had a cut and several scratches. Red, raw, they looked fresh. Since I last saw him, he had lost much weight. I could tell from the hollowness in his cheeks and from the slackness given by his shirt. "Let me sit you up," I said. An ammoniac smell hung about his face. I winced. "Your face, Uncle," I said, "smells of piss." His nostrils twitched.

"Yeah. From my head to my butt, eh?" His beard, longer now, felt like a woolly wad when I wiped his face. "Woman's piss," he said and shook his head.

"What?"

"She pissed on me." He grinned as if amused. I felt disgusted. "I had a seizure last night. That came after I ate that monkey meat. Good thing I didn't die. I woke up and she was sitting on my face and watered me with her holy water. For heaven's sake I felt cold sober after that."

I told him perhaps her quick thinking might have bailed him out of danger. He nodded. For the first time I noticed in his jet-black hair the gray hair had started showing through here and there. I could hear his stomach growl again. "I brought you leftovers—rice and liquor," I said. He asked me to dump the leftover liquor into the rice. Obliging him, I stirred the concoction, a tart smell of stale liquor and tofu. I spoon-fed him. He slurped and swallowed. He didn't even chew. I asked him how he could eat anything like this, and he spat out some rice and said, "There comes a time when you'd eat anything given you. In the South once we had no salt for weeks so we ate ash. Not a bad substitute." He hiccupped. "Be adaptable, young man."

"Where'd she get the monkey meat from?" I asked him.

"From a baby monkey, fallen off a tree and drowned in a flood. Well, she and this guy were up across the Viet-Sino border on opium runs. They got caught in a flood and had to eat bamboo rats."

I recalled the man he mentioned coming to the alley and talking with her. "What if she gets caught by the border police?"

"I'd know when that day comes."

He told me she gave him the black pellets of opium whenever he had a bout of pain—the hemorrhoids, the lungs. The pain would go away. Since then, the seizures had come more than once. If she was home, she would give him liquor and that seemed to blunt the fit and, sometimes with much liquor, he would fall asleep.

"I cursed her for giving me the monkey meat," he said. "She yelled at me, 'You're a dunghill. A dunghill for me to risk my life just to earn some cash to keep all your perverted sicknesses at bay.' That woman has a sharp tongue. But she spoke the truth. Said, 'Who's going to make all your pains disappear? Doctors? Your crummy pension? That? That goes out the window in no time just to pay the helpers to clean up your filth and buy you liquor so your opium fits won't kill you. Monkey meat, *hanh*? Last time you crashed, was it monkey meat? Or was it opium? I'm an expert now on how to kill your obscene pains when you convulse on the floor like a leech, your eyeballs roll into your head, your mouth foams like baking soda. And next time when you bang your head, find a sharp corner. *Hanh*?'"

It dawned on me about his facial cuts. "You banged your head? During a seizure?"

"Broke her cactus pot and got their spines all over my face."

As I put the empty bowl away, the fermented sourness made my nose twitch. He cleared his throat, his sticky voice becoming raspy as he told me he had done his part around the house, and yet she never appreciated it. When it did not rain for days, he twice managed to crawl out to her vegetable patch and urinate among the spinach, the purslane, the fish mint. He could tell by their smells. And she could tell what he had done sometimes by the sight of the cigarette butts lying among the patch. The fish mint leaves would smell repugnant when she chewed them, then she would spit them out and daub the paste on his forehead. He would curse, shake to get rid of the slimy gob and she would say, "You get what's coming to you. It smells like your piss, doesn't it?" She loved her garden patch. Nights when it rained, the air moist and cool, he could hear raindrops pinging on the cement steps and the moistness in the air seeped through his skin. He liked the rain, for he knew rain would soak the soil in the vegetable patches. At first light the soup mint's downy hair would spark red, the crab's claw herb would glisten, the thyme, the basil would be gorged with moisture. He could tell that one of her pet plants, the yellow jasmine vine, was coming out in clusters. She'd watered it every morning from the time she brought home the seeds, allowing the pods to dry first before breaking them open, and nursed the seeds with much watering until one morning he could smell something fragrant and that was the first time it flowered. He might hear her cheerful voice, for a change, when she plucked them at dawn.

*

I didn't visit Uncle Chung until one morning I saw his wife coming into the herbal store. She was wearing a white blouse and a red scarf around her neck, and the red was redder than hibiscus. She asked for a cough prescription. Huan's father asked if Uncle Chung was having a cold or flu and if he had a whooping cough. She smiled, said it was for a sore throat. I could hear someone coughing outside the store. A man was smoking a cigarette, standing on the sidewalk with his hands in his pants pockets. Lean, dark-skinned, he was about Uncle Chung's age. His slicked-back hair was shiny with pomade. He glanced toward the store, coughed, and spat. When she met his gaze, she smiled. She had that fresh smile that showed her white glistening teeth.

I thought of that smile when I went to see Uncle Chung afterward. He wasn't on the pallet. Seeing him sitting or lying on that pallet had become a fixture in my mind. So his absence gave me pause. I went through the curtain and saw him crawling like a caterpillar toward a corner of the room where the bathing quarter stood behind accordion panels. He bumped a chair, stopped, wiggling his head as if to get his bearings. I called out to him.

"Young man?" He cocked his head back, his hair so long now it looked like a black mane.

"Why are you in here?" I went to him.

"Water."

"Where?"

"Where she bathes."

There were no pails, not even a cup, in there. Her black pantaloons were the only item hanging on a string from wall to wall. I could see water still dripping from the pantaloons' legs. Before I said anything to him, he gave a dry chuckle. "That's my water." I pictured him worming his way to where he could catch the dripping water with his mouth.

It took a while before I could move him back out onto his pallet. Though he said he hated water, he drank some from the kettle, which I poured directly into his mouth. He asked for a cigarette. I told him I was out of cigarettes and promised him when I got money I'd buy him a pack and some liquor. I brought the black caddy to the pallet.

"I'll make you a pipe, Uncle," I said, tapping the caddy.

"It's locked. You know it."

"I'm going to break the lock." I thought of the way she'd smiled at the man, feeling resentment.

"Go ahead." He grinned.

Surprised by his encouragement, I twisted the blade of my pocketknife inside the keyhole until I felt the lock snap. "I saw her at the store," I told him casually, folding the pocketknife.

"She breezed out of here this morning and I swear I could smell perfume." He tried to clear his throat, for his voice suddenly sounded strained. "Make the pipe. I need it."

Inside the caddy a jackfruit leaf lay on top of the tobacco. The leaf was no longer fresh, the blade having gone a dark yellow. He listened to my movements and mumbled something about the leaf left in there to keep the tobacco fresh. Without it, when you smoke, he said, the tobacco lacking moisture would burn dry in the throat. He asked me what she was wearing. I told him. Then remembering her red scarf, I told him that too. "Damn," he said. He brought his lips to the pipe, paused, and said, "I remember her wearing that scarf, that red scarf, only once in her life. On the day we got married." He took a heavy drag, the water in the pipe singing merrily, and then he tipped up his face and blew a cloud of smoke toward the ceiling. "Wish I had eyes to see that scarf on her this morning. Damn it. Was she with somebody?" I told him she was, adding that he must be her business partner. Uncle Chung grunted with a twisted grin. I could sense his muted pain and at the same time my still simmering displeasure toward her. "But my woman. Oh, my woman. Whenever she bathes in there, I still feel that urge to caress her full calves. Know what they remind me of, young man? The wax gourds. Those fleshy ripened gourds to sink your teeth in." He stopped snickering and drew a healthy drag, kept the smoke in his mouth as long as he could, and his eyes became slits in his bliss. I repacked fresh tobacco in the bowl, thinking wishfully of a rice liquor bottle, because I wanted to get drunk, very drunk, with him. I took one big drag with the fresh tobacco, my head buoyed, tingling, as he slurred his words, "Know something else, young man? In the South when they amputated my limbs, they said, 'Don't cry now, Sarge.' You know why? We got no anesthesia. So I had someone press her picture on my eyes and I imagined her in that red scarf and I sucked in the pain until her picture shrank with the pain and I passed out." He nodded his head up and down like on a spring and said he understood her and even felt grateful to her still being with him. He told me the night before a female cat was yowling in heat as it wandered off the garden and into their house and his wife left her cot to come out, turned on the light, and saw the cat push its bottom against his stumped leg, rubbing and purring, and his wife said, "Look at it, oh, will you look at it," and he said, "She's horny. Aren't women like that when the moon is full?" and the cat just howled, and she said, "How can I sleep with its obscene squealing? Now, now will you look at its obscene way of showing itself?" He said, "How obscene?" She told him that the cat was lying down, twitching its tail and then flinging it to the side and there it was: the slit of its genitalia, pink and swollen. Before going back to her cot, she said she was going to stuff the cat's mouth with *lá ngón*, the yellow jasmine leaves, if it didn't stop yowling. He made a snorting sound as he laughed, said it took a long time before things got quieted down, the cat now gone, but the sound of her cot creaking beyond the curtain kept him awake into the night.

I saw a pot on the doorsill, a tall wooden stake rising from its bottom, and around the stake twined the false jasmine vine. Uncle Chung's wife's pet plant. I could tell by its pretty yellow flowers.

The next morning a boy from Uncle Chung's alley ran into our store and asked Huan's father to come quickly to Uncle Chung's house. Huan's father was like a doctor in our district, where western medicine and its physicians weren't considered trustworthy. I went with him, the boy running ahead of us before we could ask him. Inside the house I saw

Uncle Chung lying facedown by the back door where the pot of yellow jasmine sat. It took me but one look to see that he had plucked nearly all the fresh leaves of the vine, and some of them were in his mouth still and some of them lay scattered over the doorsill. White foam coated his mouth and his head full of long black hair lolled to one side and in the morning light I could see the gash and the scratches on his cheek.

I knelt down, looking at his eyes, still open. I ran my hand over them, but they stayed open. Like dolls' eyes.

I wondered if he ever cried, and if he did, would there be tears?

*

A year later I left the North to go South to fight the Americans.

Many of my friends had gone South. Nobody had heard anything from them since. I asked people why none of them was ever coming back and they shushed me. Most of them my age tattooed their arms with four words, "Born North Die South." Like it would boost their morale. Most of them died—true to their tattoos—and there was no news sent home. Then I knew why. You can't win the war with damaged morale suffered by the people at home. But the messengers of death weren't a telegram but the returning wounded who eventually reached the unfortunate families with the tragic news. To hide the most demoralizing picture of the war, the government quarantined all the wounded—they were not to see their families. But that only came after they had been seen in public. And the sight of them, maimed for life, had painted a Biblical hell about the war.

The first day on the way South on the Ho Chí Minh Trail I saw camouflaged trucks heading North. It was raining. Rain fell on our nylon raincoats, fell on the open beds of the trucks. We stopped, exchanged greeting words. Then I saw human bodies, alive and packed under the cover in mottled shades of green and brown. The wounded. They had no legs. Some burned by napalm so severely they looked leprous. Rain dripped on their limbless bodies as they slept. One peek at them and I thought of a litter of dozen pigs piled in and carried to a slaughterhouse. After the trucks came the stretchers. Sticks, bamboo slapped together. Lying on them were the blind. Some had no faces. We couldn't greet them. They couldn't see us. At the tail end of the convoy were those who had one leg, one arm, some with no arms. We stood off the muddy trail, letting them pass. They struggled on their crutches finding their footing in the mud-spattered tracks the trucks left behind. The armless ones had had their raincoats tied around their waists so the wind wouldn't blow their coats away. They walked past us, huffing and puffing. Rain-smeared sallow faces. Malaria-wrecked skin. They were all bones. So they headed home. Home. Up North. I looked at them. I wasn't afraid. Just queasy.

That day I thought of Uncle Chung. One day someone going South on this trail would look at me heading North. I might not then have a face. Likely. Or limbs. Just like Uncle Chung.

A Bridge Behind

The sun was above the bamboo grove when they reached a jetty. The day was humid. The old man paid the boat owner and, cradling one of his twin infant grand-daughters in his arms, climbed up the bank. Trailing him, his widowed daughter carried the other twin on her back. They walked toward a thatched hut with pots and pans hanging on its earthen wall. The owner was a middle-aged woman whose dimpled smile welcomed them at the entrance. The old man asked if they could catch a ferry later in the day to the next town, where they could board a bus to Hue. Then he asked how close they were to the town being captured by the Viet Cong. Half a day ahead, the owner said, then pointed to the other hut, also a food stand, from where the sound of radio drifted. She told him the radio news just announced that the South Vietnamese troops had taken the town back before dawn. She added that they usually sent out a mop-up when they recaptured a town.

While the woman served them steamed rice and fresh coconut milk, the old man pointed to his feet and asked the woman if she had an extra pair of thongs. One of his own was torn. She came back with a pair of black rubber flip-flops, bigger than his feet. He paid her for those and the meal. She clutched the money against her chest, looked up to the lanky old man, and bowed. Embarrassed, the old man bowed back.

"I'm going to the river to wash myself," the old man said to his daughter as he placed the infant in her arms. He picked up his bag and stood over her. "Can you handle both of them?"

She nodded. "Yes, Father."

He finished his bowl, swigged down his coconut milk, and slipped his feet into the new thongs. At the bank, a boat docked and let off a long line of passengers. Some went into the other food stand and some walked into the hamlet in their indigo shirts and black pantaloons. Bare-headed, canvas bundles slung on shoulders. All men. They saw him, stopped, looked, then walked on.

The old man took off his thongs and stepped into the water, which was warm and brown. He splashed water on his face, his neck and thought of taking off his shirt when suddenly magpies flew out from the trees, their legs yellow in the sun. Then gongs sounded noisily deep in the hamlet and voices screamed, "Airplane! Airplane!"

He clambered up the bank, gongs beating, men shouting. Then he heard a steady drone. Two South Vietnamese Skyraiders came into view over the hamlet so low he could see the pilots. The planes swooped down and bombs fell on the hut where they had just eaten their meals. The first explosion knocked him to the ground. Gravel, dirt, and straw flew through the air, trees snapped noisily. The second explosion was nearer and the ground beneath him burst upward, mortar and stone and leaves blowing up in a thick cloud. He shook with the ground, felt dirt in his mouth. His ears hurt. The planes roared across the river and droned away.

He stood up. Both the huts had disappeared. He saw the long wooden table shattered, its legs blown off. He saw bodies in the second hut, men in indigo shirts plastered to the ground. He screamed his daughter's name as he ran. "Phuong! Phuong!" His shouts were lost in the general uproar in the hamlet. Something on the ground whimpered. He saw a head above the ground, the owner was buried in the earth. Her face was caked with red dirt. Clods stuck in her hair. He dropped to his knees. Then he saw the tops of the infant girls' heads barely above ground and he scraped and scratched with his fingers until they bled. He sprung up, looked around until he found a branch. He plunged the stick into the dirt. It snapped. He grunted, took out his pocket knife and stabbed at the dirt around the owner's head until he loosened some and swept it off and stabbed the ground again and again. He scooped dirt by the handful and tossed it away until her face appeared. Her eyes opened. When her shoulders were free, he began to pull her up. She struggled for a time before she broke free. All the time she was holding both infants against her chest. The old man dusted their heads, relieved to see their eyes flutter and slowly open.

Just as the old man took one infant from her arms, he asked, "Where's my daughter? Where is she?"

"Over there!" The owner pointed to the other hut, then told him she had looked after the infants while his daughter went to the other hut to buy food for her babies.

The old man ran to the other hut. He saw shreds of indigo cloth, the mutilated bodies. In the hot sun he stood over the wreckage and his knees shook. The owner's cry resounded in his head.

*

The old man didn't know what to call the baby girls. They were barely two months old and so perfectly alike his daughter had said to him that naming them differently seemed odd. He did not see why, but he didn't object to them not having a name for themselves in those first two months.

Already they made him miss their mother. He tended them as lovingly as she had, spending all his time with them. A month went by, long and painful with memory. Then in the last two days of the month strange faces began appearing in the village. A drought had persisted since the start of summer that dried so much water in the pond in the back of his house he could see its mossy bottom. One morning the old man went to the cistern by the side of his house to fetch water for cooking gruel and noticed it empty. He paid Miss Lai, one of his neighbors, to carry public well water to his cistern.

With the water left in the tub the old man washed his hair. He washed it once a week. Afterward, he sat on the doorstep in the sun and dozed off. Footsteps on gravel woke him. A man wearing a palm-leaf conical hat stood in front of him. He wore a short-sleeved brown shirt and black pantaloons. The old man blinked. Strange face. Someone looking for a handout?

"Yes, Sir?" he said to the stranger.

"Well, Sir," the man said, "I'm from the local National Liberation Front committee. I'm here to ask for your support for our movement. The Front needs funds to fight the Americans."

A Viet Cong. The old man frowned. "Are you a tax cadre?"

"I'm not here to collect taxes. We collect taxes only from farmers and landlords."

For a moment the old man felt relieved. But he hated the Viet Cong on taxing the poor. After breaking their backs raising crops, the tenant farmers paid their landlords and the south government three-fourths of the harvest. Then came the Viet Cong tax cadres demanding their share for the Front.

"What are you here for?" the old man asked, scratching his head.

"That you and your neighbors go to the Front's market whenever it's convened."

"I hear you, Sir."

"We'll make sure you go," the man said, nodding. "There won't be anything open at Well Market those days."

The old man hid his antipathy. Until now the Viet Cong convened markets in other villages. He had heard about local informants who pointed out any who boycotted the Viet Cong market, and interrogation sometimes ended in execution.

The man touched the brim of his hat. "The market opens this Saturday and Sunday at the riverside. Be there, Sir."

The old man watched the man go out and down the alley, his hat bobbing beyond the bear's breech hedges. What'll happen if these communists win? he thought. At least, the fighting between the Viet Cong and the Army of the Republic of Vietnam hadn't affected his village. But he'd heard that it was bad for those hamlets where salt marshes and sand dunes stretched for miles along Route One, the north-south highway the American convoys used. The Viet Cong ambushed the convoys and retreated into the hamlets surrounded by swamps and quicksand bogs. The Americans went after them and bombarded the hamlets or burned them down.

The old man grunted as he rose to his feet. Miss Lai and her fifteen-year-old daughter were carrying in buckets of well water on shoulder poles. A banana frond floated on top of each bucket, and no drop of water spilled as they strode in. The old man paid her.

Miss Lai fanned herself with her hat. "Anything else you need, Mr. Lung?" she said.

"One of these days I might need you to read tea leaves for me."

"You said you don't believe in such things."

"When your life is undisturbed, you don't worry about your fortune." The old man told her about the Viet Cong market. "How do you feel living a life of total submission?"

"I saw them this morning at the public well. They don't look very friendly."

The following day the old man had diarrhea. He suspected the well water was contaminated. He ran out of Ganidan medicine, so when Miss Lai refilled his tub he asked if she could go to town to get him the medicine. She told him not to worry about medicine. She went out to his back yard and got a handful of clay. "Go bake this real good, Mr. Lung," she said. "Then break it into chunks and mix them in boiled water. Drink it straight."

"In the name of Heaven!"

"Hardly."

The old man drank the water and got well the next day. He considered that Miss Lai might know more than the future.

*

Saturday came. The old man went to the Viet Cong market.

At the market he saw one beggar after another, and then overheard one little girl ask her mother, "Why so many beggars, Mommy?" The mother quickly said, "They're not beggars." The little girl said, "Who are they?" Her mother hushed her when they left the market. The old man, scanning the market, knew. Those beggars worked for the local authorities. They came to the market to identify the Viet Cong agents.

On Sunday, the old man visited the Viet Cong market again. He saw the beggars' corpses, each cut up into thirds, laid out in a row. Their bags, canes and palm-leaf fans were placed by their remains. On each bag, a piece of paper proclaimed in handwritten black ink: "Spy."

Many people covered their eyes and turned away.

*

Two weeks passed. One afternoon Miss Lai passed a group of men and women in brown shirts and black pantaloons going from house to house. None of them was local.

"Coming back from your meeting, eh?" Miss Lai greeted them good-naturedly.

They stared at her and walked on.

Past midnight three men came to Miss Lai's house and dragged her outside to a rice field where her grave had been dug. They asked how she knew they were returning from a meeting. Pleading that it was just her friendly way of greeting, Miss Lai cried until she lost her voice. The next day her family retrieved her body.

The morning after Miss Lai was buried, the old man returned from the burial when the morning dew was still wet on the grass. He thought of going to the market and decided to brew some tea before setting out. When he fetched water, he stood at the tub, head bent, looking down at his reflection, the still image in white hair. Then he imagined Miss Lai's face. Here was the well water she filled his tub with, week in, week out. He imagined the clanging of her metal water buckets, made from salvaged American cooking oil cans, her wet footprints trailing from the tub to the door when she left. The thought of her senseless death sickened him. A wretched fate.

Later when the sun was high over the bamboo hedges, he went to the market. From stall to stall people talked about the execution. "They'd rather kill by mistake," a man said, "than to make mistake by not killing."

"Hey, hey," another man said, "Wasn't that woman unlucky? Must've forgotten to read tea leaves for herself that day."

The old man stared at him. Then he came over and put his large hand on the man's shoulder. "Brother," he said, looking down at the fellow, who peered up at him, wide-eyed.

For a moment the old man said nothing but read the man's expression until the man mumbled, "Yes, Sir?"

The old man dropped his voice, "Has anyone in your family been killed or died a tragic death?"

The man shook his head. "I'm very fortunate, Sir. Everyone in my family is alive and well."

"How would you like to hear someone crack a joke at your family's misfortune? Say, after your wife just died from a stray bullet?"

"Are you a relative of that woman, Sir?"

"I'm no relative of her. Consider yourself lucky that I am not."

"I . . . I . . . didn't mean her no harm, Sir. Just the way I talk."

The old man nodded, turned and left. He missed Miss Lai, but beyond that he grieved for the death of his daughter. In the hot sun he took off his hat to cool his head. A thought struck him. If Miss Lai had read the tea leaves for herself that day, would she have been still alive? His lips pursed, the old man shook his head. Miss Lai died because of her good nature. Knowing what the tea leaves said wouldn't have stopped her from being nice to people. For that he was grateful as well as sad.

*

One morning at sunrise the old man waded through the pond. Folding each lotus leaf along its midrib, he carefully tilted the leaf toward its tip. The dewdrops shook like silvery beads, broke free, and rolled into the jar. When the sun felt warm on his back, he had a jarful. A drone hummed overhead. He looked up. Flying in orderly inverted Vs, a squadron of planes looked so tiny it could pass for a flock of geese.

Inside the babies cried. He hurried back in, not bothering to dry his legs. The water in the kettle was warm when he tested it with his fingers. The old man opened a can of powdered milk and shook the bottles vigorously until the yellow powder dissolved. He made two portions and sat between the baskets, watching the girls feed. They were identical, their curly hair had a sheen. They always finished their bottles at the same time. He had brought his daughter's bamboo cot alongside his own and kept the two wicker baskets on it. At night, he made sure there were no mosquitoes inside the net before he went to bed.

Six months old now, both girls were healthy, save on one occasion a week before when one had diarrhea. The old man took his neighbor's instructions, ground some Ganidan pills and mixed them with liquid extracted from brown rice. When the diarrhea slowed, he fed her rice gruel blended with crushed ginger. On the second day the diarrhea stopped. She smiled and he held her in the crook of his arm, red-eyed from lack of sleep.

Summer ended and the rainy season came. For days a cold, dry norther blew. People said a norther could parch mud, wither leaves, stunt the young and age the old. Rain came and went. The bruised sky became a murmur of rain. Gone were the chittering of birds at sunrise, the *ah-oh* of mourning doves. At night there were no sounds of peepers, frogs, nor the hooting of owls—only the sound of rain.

Upon waking one morning, the old man parted the mosquito net and groped for his sandals with his feet. The cold water shocked him. He had slept while a foot of floodwater crept in. A toad *glunked* somewhere in the house and the water lapped the legs of his cot. He couldn't find the tin can of powdered milk he always left by the bed. He waded around the house, pantaloons rolled up to his thighs, looking for it. The floodwater must have swept it away. The girls woke, talking to themselves. He stacked up wooden containers and chairs on the divan and boiled rice to make gruel.

A quick motion at the altar had the old man looking up to see a black snake with green-yellow flecks around its neck. The old man wasn't afraid; snakes often took shelter in his house during floods. He peered at the girls through the mosquito net. Their large eyes looked up at him and their arms flailed with excitement.

The old man made the gruel, chipped off a chunk of hard brown sugar and let it melt in the bowl. He sat on the cot, blew on the spoon and fed the girls. A dry scraping sound came from the altar. *That's his tail. He wants me to feed him.*

A *glunk* sounded in the stillness. A toad leapt out of a shadow and plopped into the standing water. Upon the altar the snake uncoiled and slithered. The toad jumped against the door. The snake shot its head out, shaking it in a frenzy, as it lifted the toad into the air.

A neighbor's voice called from outside, asking the old man what he wanted from the market. He waded to the door, where the snake lay still, as if drugged. Outside the wind howled and the sky was gray. Two women sat on a makeshift raft made of banana trunks tied together, floating along what used to be a dirt path.

The old man called out to them. "Mrs. Hy, can you get me some powdered baby milk?"

"I'll get it for you, Mr. Lung," came the answer on the wind, as another woman joined them, hoisting herself onto the raft.

The women had rattan baskets on their forearms and sat with their legs drawn up to their chins. All wore conical hats the color of pale wheat and the raft carried them away into the morning grayness of sky and water.

Though the flood had begun to recede, water still ran high in the creeks and along the dirt roads. The old man fed the girls, this time putting the can of powdered milk high on the altar. As the girls ate, he sat on the cot between their baskets, letting each hold his fingers. The fire crackled low. A cold draft came across the cement floor from an opening along the base of the wall near his bed. It wasn't sealed, a brick plugged the opening. Every house in the village had such an opening to let floodwater drain out. He dreaded spending days afterward scrubbing the walls and floor.

The old man lifted the teapot. He heard shouts. A man and his wife came running in, drenched from head to toe.

"Mr. Lung!" the man cried out. "Leave, now!"

Cold air blew through the open door. "What is it, Brother Hy?"

"The Americans are coming," Hy said, wiping rainwater from his eyes.

"You must leave now," Mrs. Hy said. "The girls too. Can you carry both of them?"

"I think so. Where're we supposed to go?"

"Everyone's going to Lower Gia Linh." They turned and hurried out the door. "Quick, Sir. We'll meet you at the bridge."

"The Americans are going to blow it up," Mrs. Hy cried. "We need to cross soon."

The old man looked around anxiously. The floodwater had drained, leaving red mud everywhere. He didn't know what to take. He scooped floodwater from a small dugout under his cot and shoved in the clothing trunk and his antique tea set, secured inside a wooden box. He grabbed the milk bottles, two cans of powdered milk, some baby clothes and his own and stuffed them into a jute bag.

When the girls woke and began to cry, the old man strode over and patted them until they calmed down. He tried to think, his palms tingling with nervousness. People's shouts erupted outside.

On the dirt road people scrambled through muddy water, rain blowing in gray sheets. Then car horns blared. Through the partly opened door the old man saw two armored trucks roll in on the dirt path with American foot soldiers following behind.

Heavy footfalls at the door startled him. An American black soldier stood in the doorway. He shouted at old man, "*Di, Di!*"

"I'm leaving. I'm leaving," the old man repeated.

"*Mau!*" the black soldier shouted. "*Mau!*"

The old man said, "Yes, Sir." The black soldier stared at him and then walked off abruptly. The old man slung the jute bag around his shoulder, then remembered rice. It pained him that he had nothing to store rice in. He picked up the two wicker baskets and headed out. At the altar he stopped to pray and collect the pictures of his ancestors. He looked them over and slipped them under one of the basket quilts.

He donned his palm-leaf raincoat, draped the wicker baskets with blankets and sloshed through the floodwater to the main road. People streamed out from every dirt path, babbling and screaming, household goods strapped to their backs, slung across their shoulders. Children clung to their parents. Armored trucks blocked some paths and American soldiers ran into every house, rousing people. Shots cracked like thunderclaps, then died out on the wind. The Americans were spraying the houses with gasoline and setting them on fire. Soon the hamlet roared like a giant torch. The mass of people and animals arrived at the bridge over the river that divided the upper and lower village.

American soldiers stood around their armored trucks along the bank, pointing rifles at the crowd. Others rolled metal drums of explosives off the trucks and up the bridge. People packed the bridge trying to cross, while beneath it soldiers strung wire to wrap around its pillars. The old man's head was above the crowd. He looked for the Hys but couldn't find them.

He hooked the two baskets on his forearms, hoisted them chest high and got in front of an oxcart. The crowd pushed. He raised both of his arms above the human mass and the crazed mass moved him out and out toward the railing and he tried to get his footing forward, holding down his exasperation. The river was swollen with dark water and the wind hissed, blowing rain in clumps of wet pins. The human mass pushed on, cries scattering in the swirling winds. The oxcart moved up, the angry crowd surged to get ahead of it and the old man felt himself pressed against the railing, stopped and turned his body as the oxcart rammed into him from behind. The ox's horns caught him in the back. His body pitched forward and the basket on his right arm flew off and dropped into the roiling water.

He screamed, but the sound was lost in the clamor. The basket bobbed on the current, spun several times and then became an olive-colored patch downstream.

When the explosion splintered the bridge and dropped it into the turbulent river, the old man sat by the roadside in the rain and wept.

In a Far Country

The barge arrives very late, the rain falling in gray sheets across the quay.

I wipe my face and pull my raincoat tight around me. I cough. My throat hurts. People are coming onto the quay. Bicycles and motor scooters rev in tandem in their lanes. The air smells of gasoline fumes. The wet dusk glows with the scooters' headlights. I watch for the next wave of passengers, those on foot. Waiting behind them are the big, blue trucks. Rain slants and pops on the quay, on the gray-steel hatch of the barge's liftgate. I scan the blurred faces of the passengers hurrying up the quay, nylon bags, pink, blue, in hands, jute bags slung across shoulders. They stream past me, rustling in their nylon raincoats. Here, the locals bring them along after checking the color of the sky and shapes of the clouds.

Then I see them: a girl and a white woman, both wearing wide-brimmed straw hats but no raincoats, lugging their suitcases down the hatch. They are coming toward me, as I stand to one side, hunched, on the quay's slope. I raise my hand. "Mrs. Rossi?"

The woman turns toward me. "Hello!" she says, half smiling, half wincing from the pelting rain.

I extend my hand to help her with the suitcase. Instead, her hand comes up to shake mine.

"Please, let me help," I say, reaching for her suitcase.

"Are you from the inn?" she says.

"Yes, ma'am."

"I'm terribly sorry about the delay. I thought you must've left. I'm awfully glad to see you still here."

"Yes, ma'am. May I take you and your daughter to the car?"

"Yes, of course." She smiles, wrinkling the corners of her blue eyes. She takes the girl's hand and both of them follow me to the Peugeot, parked on the ramp. She talks to the girl about getting raincoats for their stay, for monsoon season has arrived. Although wrinkled and gray, perhaps in her late sixties, Mrs. Rossi has a clear, cheerful voice.

I open the rear door. The girl says, "Thank you," as she slides onto the seat. She must be Vietnamese, slender, rather tall. Her blue jeans are notched above the ankles, and her light skin blends perfectly with her scarlet blouse, collarless, fringed white. Mrs. Rossi takes off her wet straw hat, shaking it against her leg, and says, "No one here carries an umbrella."

"People here wear raincoats when it rains," I say as she clears a wet lock of white hair from her brow.

"In Ho Chi Minh City, too?" Mrs. Rossi asks.

"Yes, everywhere."

I put their suitcases in the trunk and close it. The rain smears the windshield as I drive through the town. Shop lights flicker. Water is rising on the main street and motor scooters sloshing through standing water kick up fantails in light-colored spouts. Ho Chi Minh City. The old name is Saigon. I hunch forward to look through the smeary windshield. Rain drums the car roof. From the ferry comes the sound of a horn. Another barge is arriving.

"This looks like a badly crowded Chinese quarter," Mrs. Rossi says from the back seat.

"Very crowded, ma'am. You never see the sun when you walk the streets here."

A surge of running water against the tires shakes the steering wheel. Water is rising to the shops' thresholds; store awnings flap like wings of some wet fowl.

"Are you from here by any chance?" Mrs. Rossi asks me.

"No. Most townspeople here come from somewhere else. Drifters, ma'am."

"You too?" Mrs. Rossi asks with a chuckle.

"Me too," I say, coughing, my throat dry as sand.

"I didn't catch your name."

"Giang, ma'am."

She repeats my name. "Can you spell it for me?" Then, hearing it spelled, she says, "So it's Zhang, like the Chinese name."

"Yes, ma'am."

"I'm Catherine Rossi. My daughter is Chi Lan."

The girl offers a hello from the back seat. I simply nod. Mrs. Rossi says, "My daughter understands Vietnamese. Only she can't speak it very well."

"She must not have lived here long."

"No, she didn't. She became my daughter when she was five years old. She's eighteen now."

"You adopted her, ma'am?" I glance again at the rearview mirror and meet the girl's eyes. I feel odd asking her mother about her in her presence.

"Yes, I adopted her in 1974. Just a year before the collapse of South Vietnam. How fortunate for us!"

"You came here that year?"

"Yes." Mrs. Rossi clears her throat. "And what were you doing in '74?"

I give her question some thought, then say, "I was in the South Vietnamese Army."

"Were you an interpreter?"

"No, ma'am."

"Then you must excuse my assumption. You speak English very well. And I'm glad you do. Otherwise we'd be making sign language now."

She laughs and the girl smiles. Her oval face, framed by raven, shoulder-length hair, is fresh. Her eyebrows curve gracefully, like crayoned black. I remember a face like that from my past.

"Were you an army lifer?" asks Mrs. Rossi.

"What is that?" I ask.

"Did you spend a lifetime career in the army?"

"No, ma'am. Only a few years."

"Did you teach school before that?"

These curious Americans. "I was on the other side. A soldier of the North Vietnamese Army."

"Were you born in the North?"

"Yes."

"And then you defected to the South and joined the South Vietnamese Army?"

"Yes, ma'am."

"They have a name for those. I'm trying to remember."

Then I hear the girl say it for her: *hoi chánh.*

Mrs. Rossi seems to be deep in thought as we leave the town, following the one-lane road north toward the U Minh district. The headlights pick up windblown rain in sprays, blurring the blacktop. There is no lane divider. Along the road drenched palms toss in the wind. Wet leaves and white cajeput flowers fall onto the windshield, and the wipers sweep over them, pressing them to the glass.

"Your victors, the North communists, didn't like the *hoi chánh* very much, so I heard."

"That's true, ma'am."

"Did they treat you any differently than the regular ARVN soldiers?"

"Sometimes worse, ma'am. I was one of those."

"What happened to those like you?"

"The North communists sent us to reform camps. Very far from here."

"For how long?"

"Ten years, ma'am. Where nobody saw us."

"Atrocious," she says. "So, you were released just two years ago? 1985? Why so long?"

"Perhaps we were not reformed well enough."

The road bends around a banana grove and on the other side golden bamboo grow thick, leaning in over the road, their trunks slender and tall, glistening in the sweeping headlights.

"Are you here to visit the U Minh National Reserve, ma'am?" I ask, half turning my head toward them.

"Yes." She seems to want to say more but stops herself. "It's a long story."

I keep my eyes on the dark road, a road I know well. But on a rainy night like this, the soaked, windswept landscape loses its familiarity. We are halfway to the inn. Lit by the headlights, yellow flowers of the narrow-crowned river-hemp shrubs seem to float along the roadside.

"Mr. Giang?" Mrs. Rossi calls out.

"Yes, ma'am?" I tilt my head back.

"Is that your last name?"

"My last name is Lê."

"Leh?"

"Yes, ma'am."

"Leh Zhang. I like the way it sounds. May I call you Giang?"

"As you wish, ma'am."

"Giang, do you know this area well?"

"Not really. Any particular place that you want to visit?"

The wind whips. In its rushing sound I can hear her long exhalation.

"I came here," Mrs. Rossi finally says, "to search for the remains of my son."

"Okay," I say with a sudden tightness in my throat.

"My son served in the United States Army. 1966. 1967. He was a lieutenant."

"He died here, ma'am?"

"Yes. Somewhere here. It's been twenty years." Then she drops her voice. "His remains must still be here, I think."

"What makes you say that?"

"This is where he died, and his body was never recovered."

"How do you plan to find him? It's a vast area."

"I have a map. Someone drew it for me. Crudely, but clear enough. A fellow who served in the platoon that my son commanded."

"He saw your son die?"

"No." She pauses. "No, he didn't. But he was in the firefight. When they came upon this fellow, badly wounded, the next day, they said, 'Where is Lieutenant Nicola Rossi?' They counted all the bodies, and all were accounted for except my son."

"But nobody saw him die."

"That fellow saw him, still alive. A mortar blew up and trapped my son beneath a fallen cajeput trunk. The Cong didn't see him or he'd have been killed on the spot. They shot all the fallen men in the head. My son must've known this."

I draw a deep breath. "How would you be able to identify his remains? Unless there're some items with the bones . . ."

"That's what worries me. I pray that I'd find identification."

I say nothing, keeping my eyes on the road, lined with thin-trunked hummingbird trees.

"Are there any local guides I can hire?" Mrs. Rossi asks. "To go out and look for the remains?"

"The owner of the inn can help you." I speak with my face half turned. "She's from here."

"I much appreciate it," Mrs. Rossi says.

I want to tell her not to raise her hopes, but I can't bring myself to say it. I think of the inn owners' son. How many unclaimed remains are there in that wilderness? Dug up, displaced by rodents and wild animals. Long scattered, blown to pieces by bombs. Charred by forest fires. Time and nature are cruel.

*

I am not from here. But I know this region well. I lied to Mrs. Rossi about that.

Carrying in its womb the U Minh vast wetland forest, this region of the Mekong Delta used to be the territory of IV Corps, the southernmost of the four military corps of South Vietnam, which saw many savage fights. Although the battles may have long been forgotten, some places cannot forget.

I live and work in a roadside inn. The owner and his wife are in their late sixties. The old woman runs the inn and cooks meals for the guests. I drive to Ông Doc town, twenty kilometers south, to pick up customers when they arrive on buses, boats or barges. Most of them come to visit the Lower U Minh National Reserve, twenty kilometers north.

On the night Mrs. Rossi and her daughter arrived, the woman inn owner cooks a fat catfish and a pot of white-rice porridge. Outside it is wet and windy. I take our guests upstairs with their suitcases and, coming down the stairs, I can hear the sizzling of onions. The old woman opens the lid, sprinkles black pepper on the plump catfish just burst open, and stirs the porridge until all the black flecks disappear.

We eat with only one fluorescent lamp in the center of the oblong table, rain on the window slats. Before commencing to eat, Mrs. Rossi bows and says a prayer. The girl, too, crosses herself. The old woman pays them no mind as she ladles the steaming porridge from the pot into each bowl, breaks a chunk of the ginger-colored catfish with the ladle, then dusts the bowl with pepper.

As we eat, the old woman slurps the porridge and sniffs the steam. When she finishes, she goes to the sideboard and carries back a plate. She sits it down by the lamp and Mrs. Rossi exclaims, "Look at that! Are they longans?"

The old woman just looks at Mrs. Rossi.

"Yes," I say. "They are in season now."

Mrs. Rossi's daughter plucks one longan fruit and feels its bark-like, yellow-brown thin rind. She looks at me. "How do you say longan in Vietnamese?"

"*Nhan.*" I enunciate the word. "You've eaten it before?"

"I did. In a Vietnamese restaurant where we live."

"Where?"

"Rockville." She smiles. "State of Maryland."

"You liked it then?"

"I didn't eat it fresh. They served it in a sweet dessert."

"That's *chè*. The sweet slushy dessert."

Mrs. Rossi peels the rind and eases the fleshy white fruit into her mouth. She closes her eyes and shakes her head, murmuring. After eating a few longans, she says to me, "Would you mind telling the owner the purpose of our stay?"

*

Back then, the old woman tells us, shortly after the North and the South were reunited, people from all parts of the country journeyed to the Central Highlands and the Mekong Delta to search for the remains of lost sons, lost husbands. This region, with its vast wetland forest, was known to the North Vietnamese Army as Military Zone 9, the name borrowed from the French colonial days. You would see people at dawn heading into the woodland beyond the inn, across the grassland and rice fields, carrying knapsacks, spades. At dusk they would come back out. Some of them stayed here at the inn. Mostly civilians. Sometimes you would see soldiers, but they didn't stay at the inn. They came in organized groups—called remains-gathering crews—and they would camp in the woodland with their trucks for a week or longer. Many crew members were war veterans who had fought in Military Zone 9 and knew the region well. They remembered where they had once buried their comrades in makeshift graves. Before searching, they would burn incense and pray for the lost souls to guide them to where their remains could be found. During the war, thousands of soldiers were stationed in this region, always deep in the swamp forest. Many died from bombing and shelling and ground assaults. In that forbidden swamp, the flesh and bones of soldiers on both sides lay under the peat soil.

The old woman points toward the unseen grassland and the paddy beyond. "After the war, the people came here to settle in the buffer zone. Many were war veterans. They cleared enough land for raising crops. They burned down cajeput trees and sold the wood."

Mrs. Rossi asks me if the old woman, or any native, knows the region well enough to act as guide.

The old woman says, "I have never been to the swamp forest myself. I have no business going in there. It is haunted." She says that on rainy nights following a humid day when the swamp vapors are thick, some in the buffer zone say they can hear human sounds from deep in the forest. If you listen, they say, you can hear the human screams and sobs, the wind-born wails coming and going sometimes until first light.

Mrs. Rossi asks me, "Do you think anyone would be available for hire?"

"Yes," I say. "They will do whatever you want."

"I have the map. I think that'll help."

"I think it will."

But deep down I know it won't.

During my time with the North Vietnamese Army, we buried corpses under giant trees to shelter the graves from bombing. Flies, wind, sand, and graves. Graves everywhere. Graves we had dug to bury the dead and sometimes to rebury the dead when bombs fell on them again. In time, weeds and creepers overgrew the graves. Then you could no longer tell if they were there at all. Sometimes, though, you could spot a grave from the familiarity of the surroundings, perhaps from a marker you had planted at the grave site, or from a tree shorn by bombs that still stood in its odd-looking shape. Then you would unearth the grave only to find nothing but bones. Always bones because termites had eaten everything else. Whatever was left was gripped and twined with tree roots so tight the bones broke. Carefully you would unknot the roots one by one, so the bones wouldn't snap, the skull wouldn't crack. But it was always bones. When you held a fragment of bone in your hands, or a skull marred with spiderweb cracks, you couldn't tell if it was Vietnamese or American.

*

Mrs. Rossi and I go into forest for the first time, in a sampan. There are four of us. Mrs. Rossi and me, Old Lung and Ông Ba. Old Lung was a war veteran like me. A prisoner of war, he was sent to a reform camp, but only for three years. Unlike me, he had fought for the Republic of Vietnam. Most people settling in the buffer zone are soldiers' widows and war veterans. Former North Vietnamese Army soldiers, former Viet Cong fighters. Enemies of the former Republic. Old Lung had fought both the Viet Minh in the Indochina War and the Viet Cong and NVA in the Vietnam War. He is like a mongrel among the others. He lives in a hut in the buffer zone. Old Lung found Ông Ba, a settler who owns a fifteen-foot-long sampan fitted with a Kohler outboard motor, the type that has become ubiquitous in the water grid here for many settlers who own a canoe or a sampan; you can never find them in the waterways without a motor.

We follow Bien Nhi Canal, going east. The canal was arrow straight and clear with a paved road edging it on one side, with dwellers' homes on the other side, mirrored in the blue water. Ông Ba said it was an elephant road before he was born—trampled down by traveling herds to become a path—and whenever there was a dirt path there were migrators.

When the sun finally breaks through on the water's surface, we enter Cái Tàu River, the waterway wide and brown. There are fish stakes pounded into the riverbed along the banks. We reach Trem River and turn south, seeing the forest on the far right, green with white flecks of cajeput flowers.

Past a sawmill there are lumber barges moored along the low-lying bank. Ông Ba says, "Yonder it is." He turns right into a canal, the sampan bobbing on the choppy currents where the canal enters the river, the banks high and thick with bear's breeches, glossy- and spiny-leaved, and over the bank you can see the sawmill's brown roof.

When we no longer hear the noises from the sawmill, at least a kilometer behind, Ông Ba brings the sampan alongside the bank where it flares into a shaded cove. Ahead one hundred yards is the forest.

"This is the place," Ông Ba says, cutting off the motor.

I translate for Mrs. Rossi. Old Lung simply watches her. She looks at the hand-drawn map and then across the grassy tract of land, brown in the sun. She gestures toward the open space: "I imagine the American Army base used to be over there?"

"Yes, ma'am," I say.

She tilts back her umbrella, her face full of sun, and gazes into the shadowy space farther downstream where the canal disappears into the forest.

Old Lung opens his knapsack and takes out a cigarette. In the rucksack he carries his lunch packed in a plastic container, a bottle of water, and a large bundle of clear nylon. He lights the cigarette, works the knapsack onto his back, and picks up the machete and the long-handled spade with a small blade.

I borrow the map from Mrs. Rossi. In the hand-sketched map the U Minh forest is kidney-shaped, bisected by a river running north-south. From the confluence, the map says, where Cái Tàu River flows into the Trem, you go north for fifteen kilometers, and there you see the old American Army base sitting westward from the Trem River.

"You've done this before," I speak to Old Lung. "How will you go about it with her?"

"You want to hear the truth?" Old Lung glances at me. "I helped many folks looking for bones. But they're our own people. They're poor and tough, who can put up with hardship and the forest scourge. Still in the end many of them gave up and went back home. They got ill, and there's no infirmary in this buffer zone. You have to go to Ông Doc town for medical treatment." He squints at me. "How long can she last? How much faith does she have? It's a vast area and it's only me and her."

"I know it's a vast area, but I already told you about her son. He was last seen here." I point toward the map of the forest. "If he made it out of the base and into the forest, he wouldn't get very far before the Viet Cong picked him up. There's a creek not far after you enter the forest, and on the other side of that creek are swamps with bogs and many spots of quicksand. If I were you, I'd stay on the one side of that creek that's safe and work your way down."

"I've seen that creek. I believe it goes to the sea several kilometers toward the west."

"Good. It's a lot of land to cover, but not too vast. You do your best, old man, and I trust you."

Old Lung clears his throat and scratches his head. "I should tell you this. There's a woman who works as a medium for folks who came here looking for bones. She lives in our buffer zone and you should see her backyard. It must have more than two dozen graves from the bones she collected by helping those folks search that forest and elsewhere. Unidentified bones that nobody wanted. But that woman has a good heart. She took the bones home, washed them with five-flavor berry leaves, wrapped them in nylon sheets, and buried them, each set of bones in a grave. She put flowers on every grave."

"You mean to tell me that the bones could be anywhere, even in that woman's backyard?"

"Yeah." Old Lung taps his spade. "But I must start somewhere, right? You know why I don't carry a spade with a wider blade? This dry season makes the clay soil in there hard as rock and you must use a spade with a small blade. You dig and sparks fly. Eh?"

His machete will help him clear the bushes and branches from giant bamboo and ebony. But he has no help. When the remains-gathering crews go into the forest, they survey the area for half a day and then start digging. At night they hang hammocks and sleep in the forest. It takes weeks; sometimes they find nothing, other times they stumble upon a mass burial ground.

I hand the map back to Mrs. Rossi. "I wish I could go into the forest with you, ma'am. But I'm needed back at the inn. Mr. Lung knows the method. He has a good plan."

"You mean he knows where to look?" Mrs. Rossi asks.

"And how to spot a makeshift grave. Like a hump of earth above the ground. Things like that. I can find more men to help, if he finds that he can't dig by himself anymore."

"I understand, Giang," Mrs. Rossi says. "I understand perfectly."

*

Rain. Falling on the inn's red-tiled roof, which slants sharply over the veranda. Sluicing over the low-hanging edge of the roof, glittering in a white-water curtain. The veranda, deep and always shadowy even on a sunny day, surrounds the inn, shielding the first-floor rooms from the pelting rain. Bundled up in my raincoat, I quick-step onto the veranda and set down the two bags of groceries and household supplies next to the entrance door.

It's noon. The rain hasn't let up all day. Water started rising on the roads on my way back from the town. On a day like this, Mrs. Rossi stays home.

We also have new guests who arrived at the inn three days ago. A couple from Ireland. They drove down from Ho Chí Minh City. The husband is a journalist. Since their arrival he has gone around the U Minh region, always with a camera, backpack, and palm-sized voice recorder. The wife, in her late thirties, made friends easily with us. When she first heard of the purpose of Mrs. Rossi's visit, she said to her, "Jasus, ye break my heart."

On the rear veranda, Mrs. Rossi and Maggie, the Irish woman, are scrubbing clothes in a round rubber tub. The inn owner normally does this chore. Though old, she can still scrub and wring garments with her small hands. At times she would tread on them the old-fashioned way, while hoisting the legs of her pantaloons.

"Giang," Mrs. Rossi calls to me, "you're back already."

Maggie, her face wet, raises her voice with a toss of her head. "Made it back in one piece in this bloody weather, didn't ye?"

"Roads are flooded now," I say to them. "Where's your husband, Maggie?"

"Went to meet his local guide and then off to the jungle." She means the U Minh forest. "I said go aisy on a day like this. He's beyant control. Wouldn't you say, Catherine?"

Mrs. Rossi shrugs. I step closer and look at her lower legs. Above her ankles are crowds of deep purple marks like she has been hit with a buckshot.

"Leech bites?" I ask her, pointing at them.

"How d'you know by just looking?" asks Mrs. Rossi.

"I've got scars on my legs from them." I pull up my trousers legs. The women and Chi Lan stare at the pea-sized scars on my shins and calves.

Her face scrunched up, Chi Lan shakes her head. "You got them during the war, *Chú*?"

"From years in the jungle."

Mrs. Rossi drops a wrung-out sock into an empty basket next to the tub. "Every night when I take off my socks, they're bloodstained from those suckers. The first few days in the forest I was near tears from putting up with them. Mr. Lung, he seemed unperturbed by leeches and bugs. You know how he got rid of those leeches for me?"

"With his cigarettes?" I ask. "Make them drop away?"

"That or I just pulled them off my legs."

"That's why you've got scars like these." I sit down on my heels and put my fingertip on her calf. "Do like this. Slide your fingernail under the sucker's mouth. It'll break off. Won't leave any scar mark on you, I guarantee."

"Is there any way to keep them from latching on to you?"

"I'll get you some chopped tobacco. Soak your socks in the tobacco water and then dry the socks before putting them on. Leeches won't bother you again."

"Does it really work?"

I nod. "Or you can cut the leech in half."

Looking at me, Mrs. Rossi leans back slowly and smiles. "But it'll regenerate itself, won't it?"

"No, ma'am. Mother Nature is fair to us that way."

Mrs. Rossi pats my hand. "You're a kind soul, Giang. I know yesterday was your day off, and you volunteered to go with me into the forest to help Mr. Lung. Bless your heart. I'm thankful for this torrential rain that keeps us from going out."

Maggie laughs. "*Zhang*, people like you will do us all the good in the world, won't you?"

She rises with the tub in her arms and empties it over the edge of the veranda, then refills the tub with rainwater sluicing like waterfall from the edge of the roof. I have seen her and Chi Lan washing with rainwater, cleaning and scrubbing themselves until their faces glowed. Precious rainwater. When it rains I would fill jugs of it for the old woman to wash and bathe the old man, and for cooking and drinking too. Once, while filling the jugs, I told Chi Lan that in the jungles we soldiers used to wait for rain so we could shower, and sometimes it was just a passing shower which stopped before we could get all the suds off our bodies. She laughed.

"Is she sleeping?" Chi Lan looks back into the house for the old lady.

"She's feeding him," I say.

"You want me to fill the water jugs for her?"

"No." My hand touches my shirt pocket where the cigarette pack is. "We have all we need for now."

I catch her gaze at my gesture for a smoke. I leave my hand on my chest. She squats down and begins scrubbing a mud stain off her mother's jeans in the tub.

Mrs. Rossi arches her back, drawing a deep breath. "I must say I admire the old lady for washing clothes like this. My back is killing me already."

Maggie is wringing her denim shirt until veins bulge on the backs of her hands. "That's why that oul' lady walks bowlegged." She shakes out the shirt loudly. "Mother o' God give us a washer and a dryer. That's one thing we need here."

I have told them to air-dry their clothes in the sun once a week, so the sun would kill any eggs that might have been deposited in their garments. The books they brought with them too. Shake them out once in a while. On the first day of their arrival I heard her scream upstairs. I saw a trail of black ants that led into their room and heard her say to Alan, her husband, "I wouldn't even give them the steam of my piss." So I went in and there I saw a dead scorpion under the dresser. I picked it up and told them I would get rid of the ants for them. "Oh, you're a treasure," she said. "Please make them bloody eejits go 'way."

Now Maggie hangs up her shirt on the cord strung across the veranda and clips it with a wooden clothes-peg. In her late thirties, she is lean, small-bosomed, her sandy-blonde hair tied into a ponytail. Bony in the face that's freckled heavily under the eyes, clear blue eyes, she smiles a lot, the ear-to-ear smile that brings a smile to your face, too. She comes back to the tub for her cotton slacks. "You ever got caught with this sorta rain in the jungle while ye go about yeer business?" she asks Mrs. Rossi.

"Oh, I've been in those downpours and the misting after the monsoon rains. It's miserable, Maggie."

"Tell me, love, how on earth can ye find anything in such a place? In that wilderness God doesn't plant a sign that says, 'Dig here!' Ye know what I mean."

Mrs. Rossi skims the suds off Chi Lan's forearm with her finger. "Mr. Lung has a method," she said. "We kinda divided up the area and went from one section to the next. When we spot a mound of earth here and there, he'd dig and dig, bless his old heart. He never stops going until I beg him to take a breather. Then he'll take a sip of water, have a smoke, and then be back at it. Most of the time we find nothing. A few times we found bones, human bones, and God Almighty I'd feel myself shaking. And you know something? You can't tell one skull from another. They all look like they were cast from the same mold. Those unclaimed skulls belong to unknown soldiers and that's why somebody like me is still searching for them."

Listening to Mrs. Rossi, I couldn't help thinking the same thought. You can't tell those skulls apart. You can't tell a Vietnamese skull from an American skull.

Mrs. Rossi shakes her head, as if trying to chase away something unpleasant. "One time we found a penicillin bottle among the bones. It was closed tight with a rubber cap. Mr. Lung opened it and there's nothing but a piece of paper inside. Well, he doesn't speak English like you, Giang, but after a lot of gesticulating and with much pidgin English, he got me to understand that it had to do with a soldier's identification. Things like name, combat unit, rank, birthplace, and hometown. He said that back when the remains-gathering crews would arrive, searching for the remains of their comrades, the bones they found without penicillin bottles would be brought back and buried in the National Military Cemetery in Ho Chi Minh City. The unidentified bones would be interred in the section for the remains of unknown Vietnamese soldiers."

Maggie frowns. "The Americans must've bombed the bejesus outa the jungle. So what's left in there to find?"

I cut in. "Sometimes all you rebury are a few bones. The rest got blown away."

"And if ye find them," Maggie asks, "how d'ye take them oul' bones back?"

I plug a cigarette in my mouth without lighting it. "They pack them in nylon bags and hang them on tree limbs. Keep them away from termites because the remains-gathering crews would stay in the forest for weeks. They bring all the bags back to the cemetery when their stay is over."

Maggie screws her eyes at me. "Say ye stumble on a skull of an orangutan. Can ye tell? Or ye bag it up and bury it in your National Military Cemetery among the oul' souls of yeer soldiers?"

Mrs. Rossi eyes Maggie with a bemused expression. I take the cigarette from my lips. "The men of the remains-gathering crews know about bones. They know how to tell a monkey skull from a human skull. A woman's skull from a man's skull . . ."

"Seriously?" Maggie chirps up.

"Yeah," I say. "They can tell. A woman's chin bone is smaller than a man's chin bone. The eye sockets are deeper. That sort of thing."

"Ah, now," Maggie says, nodding. "Nurses, weren't they?"

"Soldiers. Women fighters."

Mrs. Rossi wipes foam off Chi Lan's cheek. "We did find a couple of skulls and Mr. Lung said they were women's skulls. I had not the faintest idea why he said that. But women soldiers?"

I told them the women's skulls must have belonged to a vanguard unit of women fighters who took risks to spearhead into enemy territory. That was their mission. All of them were women.

Maggie whistles. "All women, eh? Aw for Jaysus sake . . ."

Mrs. Rossi sighs. "Mr. Lung was respectful with the bones we found. You must see how careful he was with them when he came upon them . . ."

"He's a gravedigger and undertaker around here," I say.

"I admire him for his professionalism," Mrs. Rossi says, "but more so for the personal feeling in the way he treated the bones. Before he dug, he'd light a stick of incense. Then you just watch him stab and stab the ground with his shovel and sometimes it'd hit rocks and sparks'd fly and then he suddenly stopped and looked down and there lay a small bundle in the hole, just a nylon bunch tattered and gray and when he ran his hand over it, the nylon fell apart. Like ashes. A skull cracked and chipped. Like broken china."

"What'd he do with them?" Maggie asks. "In the name of Jaysus, Mary and Holy Saint Joseph!"

Mrs. Rossi's voice drops. "He rewraps the bones in a clean piece of nylon he brought with him and shovels dirt over the pit and says a prayer."

I feel as if she's living her wish through Old Lung's acts, to see her son's remains ever cared for by a stranger in an unknown place.

Mrs. Rossi continues, "After he reburies the bones, sometimes with a skull, Mr. Lung flattens the dirt and removes the incense stick. I asked him why he did that and he explained, while miming, that'd wipe out any sign of a grave. 'Why,' I asked. 'So the bad people wouldn't come upon it,' he said. That's as far as I could get to the truth."

Her wrinkled face holds a dogged patience. "Mr. Lung did the right thing," I say. "There are bone crooks who go around digging up bones and selling them."

"Selling bones?" Mrs. Rossi's mouth falls agape.

"Swindlers. Bone profiteers."

"Selling bones to whom?" Mrs. Rossi asks.

"To contractors who build the National Military Cemetery."

"I might be obtuse," Mrs. Rossi says. "Would you please explain *that*?"

"These bone crooks go into the forests. The worst of them follow the poor folks after they've recovered the bones of their relatives and outright rob them. Then they sell the bones to the contractors in the city. You see, ma'am, for each tomb the contractors build, they charge the government. The more tombs the more profit. The contractors divide up the bones they buy from the bone crooks, and instead of building one tomb for a dead soldier's bones they build two, three tombs and charge the government. For the unknown remains, they'll end up having several unknown markers for one dead soldier. But the worst, ma'am, are those who rob the relatives. Instead of being properly buried back home with a tomb and a headstone, a dead soldier will be buried in the National Military Cemetery as an unknown soldier with his bones in multiple tombs."

Maggie taps her forehead. "Aw, Gawd, I sure never heard of this meself."

"Me neither," Mrs. Rossi says. "Who could think of such an inhuman thing?"

Chi Lan, kneeling, wraps her arm around her mother. "Mom, it's all right."

I ask Mrs. Rossi softly, "Was there a girl in your son's life before he went to Vietnam?"

"Not that I know of. I think that might've been the Lord's

blessing for him, because when you're in love, you dream of a home and someone might end up with a broken heart, a broken dream."

"Wouldn't it have been a joy if your son and Chi Lan met?"

"Oh, stop it, Giang." Mrs. Rossi laughs, a scratchy laugh. I gaze at her wrinkled face as she tosses her head back, fanning her face with her hand. *Why a Vietnamese adopted child?* Did it let her mother hold on to the memory of her lost son? I like Mrs. Rossi. A retired high school principal, a sweet old lady. I admire her determination to find her son's remains. More so, I admire her faith. Still strong after twenty years.

The River of White Water Lilies

Dear Mamma,

I'm writing to you from our base camp. It was once a French fort during the Indochina War. From the rear of the base looking west I can see the U Minh forest beyond the perimeter of barbed wire. At first light the leaves of the forest are bright green and there are trees covered in white flowers, but in the heat haze of the day the leaves turn a dusty green and the flowers wither and fall in the monsoon rain. Past the base's entrance I can see the little Viet town. A red-dirt road runs through the middle of it and the spreading crown of a chinaberry shades the refreshment shack. We call this little town "Blind Colony," Mama. It's the same age as the base built a few years ago. Like parasitic climbers on old tree trunks. And the sight of our star-painted trucks is as familiar as the sight of the old Lambretta minibus that comes chugging in every day at daybreak, unloading bags of fresh onions in front of the refreshment store, and returning before sunset to collect them onions now neatly diced. They must have good soil somewhere to grow those onions, for each bulb is big and smooth and shiny, and those bulbs could stay fresh for a few months. You know why, Mama? After they are harvested and dried, those who grow them preserve them in DDT and gypsum powder so fungi and onion flies and eelworms would keep off them. Otherwise the onions would rot in a week. Now the Viet women would receive bags of them at first light and all day long slave dicing up them onions. At day's end, eyes teary and red when their bags are filled with diced onions, they must have wiped their eyes a hundred times. Before long, their eyesight is affected by the DDT and eventually they go blind.

Beyond the town is the Trem River. That's what the Viets call it. We follow that river north on our patrols. Sometimes we stay out for days on end guarding the villages that lay hidden in the banana and bamboo groves along the river. There's a Catholic village that lies beyond the riverbank, deep in the forest. On quiet evenings, if you stand amongst the huts, you can hear the sound of waves coming from the western sea.

We protect that Catholic village against the enemy. The villagers are northerners who escaped the communist terror in 1954 when Vietnam was divided into North and South. The mammas and grandmas bake dumplings and steamed buns and we eat them and thank God that we don't have to eat our ham and lima beans. We give them our C-ration cans in return. The village militia have lookouts in the forest and along the river, and they communicate with one another using Morse code through their hand-held radios. They have M1 Garand and carbine rifles. We gave them M-16 rifles and mortars.

One night their scouts spotted the Viet Cong's movement toward their village and sent their men the coordinates through Morse code. They fired their mortars. They got the Viet Cong just as they were crossing the river. When it was over, canteens, rubber shoes and bodies floated on the water. In the morning the river had carried away the blood, but the mud along the riverbank was soaked red and the fish were fighting one another for the human flesh caught between the battered-looking paling.

*

Mama, today is my birthday. The ides of October. I have been here ten months and twenty one days. Many of us here are my age or younger. We are young men in the body and aged in the soul. I was twenty-two when I came to Nam and now, after turning twenty-three, I am lost in this god-forsaken land.

*

I don't know these people. I don't know their language. I don't know what they think. They smell strange. Talk strange, like chipmunks. They always smile, Mama. They smile as we leave a village and then one of our men lost his foot in the paddy. In this vill I saw these old hags with blackened teeth and bloody mouths. You should see them, Mama. They have snaggleteeth and they keep spitting red spit all over the place. One of my men said to me, Have you heard of betel nut? I said no. He said back home we chew Skoal, Red Man, here they chew betel nuts. I said No thanks. They look repugnant to me. I saw bomb shelters in their huts. They hide children in there. This old hag sat in the bunker with two tiny kids. Just plain naked. Her lips were swollen red from chewing betel nuts, and she was cracking lice from the kids' hair with her teeth. You can hear the lice pop. There was a rice pot on the dirt floor. Cooked over wood fire. Another pot of greens boiled in water. Ian Vaughn, our point man, gave her a can of ham. She just looked at him. You often see that same look on their dumb-eyed buffalos. So he left it on the floor by the rice pot. We can't talk to them, Mama. We don't know how. The four words we know when we command them to do what we ask are *di di*, that's go away, and *dung lai*, that's halt! If they don't, we'll shoot. Before we entered this vill, we saw someone slinking away in the woods. Ian called *dung lai!* The figure kept running so Ian opened up. The figure hit the ground. We came up and found a ten-year-old boy.

*

The first time I saw a Viet kid, perhaps six years old, he was squatting on his heels, with blood caked on his skinny legs. He had an olive-colored can of ham in one hand and a Sterno heat can in the other. With a piece of wood, he wedged open the lid of the Sterno can. A matchbox lay at his grimy foot. He lit a match, touched it to the paste and shrank back when a blue flame spurted. He put four pebbles on the rim of the Sterno can and placed the unopened can of ham on them. I picked up the ham can and opened it with my P-38 on my dog-tag chain. He lifted his face to look at me. His eyes were peppercorn black. His gaze followed my hand.

*

Dear Mamma,

I want to tell you about the Trem River. It runs North-South through the U Minh forest, cutting it in half. One day, on a river craft patrolling near a creek called Ra Ghe, I saw white flowers floating along the riverbank. For some ten miles all I could see were myriad rows of flowers whitewashing the edge of the water. They were floating on leaves that are notched deeply down the center and look like human hearts. The fragrance followed us upriver until the river bends and then the white flowers and their scent disappeared. When I mentioned them to the colonel, he said, "Do you know what the Viets call that stretch of the river? *The River of White Water Lilies.*"

The Trem changes its colors with the seasons; brown-red during the monsoon when the cajeput forests bleed into the creeks and canals, and then opaque white during the dry season when silt at the river mouth comes inland with saltwater. At night when we patrol the river we often see fishermen out on the water in their sampans, each hung with a lantern on the stern and on the bow. The lanterns make the river smell of smoke, and the water glows with their reflections. I've been told that the fishermen go out to catch prawns. Not the ordinary prawns but tiger prawns. Mamma, they are at least ten inches long, rusty-brown with black-and-white bands across their humpbacks.

*

Dear Mamma,

Some of the boys aren't cut out for this place. We were out on patrol a few days ago. It was a hazy morning. We were wading single file across a canal that hugged the side of a Viet village. The bank was bolstered against erosion by a thick barrier of bamboo. Where the hedge ended, I could see the soil so fretted away by water that the bamboo roots were exposed. Brown thatch roofs peeked out between the green leafage. Suddenly a figure slunk out from behind a clump of reeds. A kid. He was lugging a rifle. Ian Vaughn, our point man, hollered, "Hey! Who goes there?" The kid turned, looked back. Then he bolted. A gunshot rang out and the kid fell. Sergeant Sunukkuhkau lowered his M-16 as Ian climbed the bank and walked into the tall reeds. The kid's wound was still leaking blood like thick nail varnish. Sarge picked up the kid's gun. An old battered Thompson submachine gun. Its walnut-brown buttstock was badly nicked and chipped. To look at the old faded thing you'd think it had been buried in a paddy since World War II.

Sarge turned on Ian.

"*Who goes there?* What in the name of God were you thinking?"

Ian looked down at the lifeless body.

"He was just a kid, Sarge."

"And this?" Sarge thrust the old Thompson against his chest. "A wooden toy?"

"Maybe they made him do it." Ian looked into Sarge's eyes then quickly looked away. "Told him to shoot at us."

"May I ask," Sarge tapped the twenty-round box magazine, "what would have happened if he had emptied this on us?"

Ian said nothing.

After that patrol we were ordered to move into enemy territory and told to lock and load. The man next to Ian doubled back and talked to

Sergeant Sunu. Before long, Sarge came up the line and poked his finger at Ian's M-16.

"Remove the magazine."

"Why?" Ian said.

"I want to see it."

Ian pressed the magazine release. It fell out and before he could feel it in his hand, Sarge had seized it. One peek into the magazine and he grabbed Ian by the collar of his shirt. "This," he said, shaking the empty magazine in Ian's face, "is unthinkable. Someone from our side could've paid a dear price for this. You don't want that on your conscience, do you, boy? You kill the slopes or get killed. Simple as that."

Slopes, gooks, dinks. Every war slogan inked across a banner in the barracks back home has one of those words. The "Kill-a-Cong" posters are a favorite among the new recruits.

*

Dear Mamma,

I'm not sure how long we've been stationed on the riverbank near the Catholic village now. Some days there isn't much to do. It seems we're always waiting. Waiting for the worst. There's this girl in the village. A schoolteacher, I think. Her name is Lan. Sometimes I take her up on the 10-ton thunder truck, sitting on its bed mounted with a quad-50 machine gun. The kids always wave and smile at the truck as it rolls through the rows of huts and the adults stand in muted admiration at the sight of the quad-50 draped with an American flag. Late afternoons sometimes the men test the quad's maximum range and I sit with Lan on the bank to watch the streaks of red tracers. Every living Viet in the village comes out of their hooch to watch the fireworks.

Lan speaks good English. I told her that it always pinches my gut when the quads go into action. She asked why and I said that it means some souls in the bush are in trouble. She said I have a good heart and I told her I always carry the Bible with me, even when I'm out on patrol. She's a Catholic, too, and we study the Bible together. She's teaching me Vietnamese. I asked her if I could teach English to her students. Now the children perk up at the sight of me, the red-haired American who has to stoop in the low-ceilinged classroom. My off-tone pronunciation of tricky Vietnamese words always gets them giggling.

Lan tells me the secret is to relax your jaw.

She asked me one day about Christians in America. "I heard that the sects are split into black congregations and white congregations over there."

"We have Presbyterians, Episcopalians, Baptists, Methodists and lots of others. Of course, the Baptists are divided into sects of their own. We have Shakers, Quakers, Mormons, Lutherans, and only God knows how many more."

Lan just about fell over laughing at all the names.

Once, after school, one of the children took me by the hand and led me to their home. I was invited to sit on a rush mat on the packed dirt floor to eat their food. First, I worked my feet out of my heavy boots so I could sit like them with my legs cross-folded into each other. I guess it takes time for limbs to adapt. But it doesn't take long for the tongue to acquire a taste for boiled vegetables, poached fish, and rice. They eat a lot of fish, cabbage, and sweet potatoes here. At every meal there's a crockpot of *canh*, their soup, with pumpkin and baby shrimps. I wish you could taste the *nuoc mam*, their fish sauce. We ate quietly as dusk fell and then I bid them farewell and made my way back to camp. I could hear the deep-throated *cu-ckoo-cu-ckoo* of a bird call echoing mournfully across the water and the swamp. Every evening the Viets burn cajeput leaves to keep the mosquitoes away. I stood there for a minute looking out over the river and the bitter-smelling smoke made my eyes teary.

*

Dear Mamma,

They let their chickens roam about here and the bright red of a rooster's comb is the red I see in my mind when I think of the village. It makes me feel peaceful.

We had to teach the kids how to open the C-ration cans with P-38 can openers. I wish you could have seen the children taste our food for the first time. Most of them paused when they took a mouthful of spaghetti and meatballs and some even spat it out. I made Lan try the beans and franks. She took the hot dogs, cut them up, fried them with onions and ate them with white rice. It tasted much better that way. I've been to her house on several occasions. Her father is the village chief, a cultured white-haired man who comes from a mandarin family in the North. The first time I entered the anteroom he was sitting in a chair with his feet planted on the floor, his hands resting on his thighs. He never crossed his legs. I considered myself fortunate that I sat like them, for later she told me that one of the Viet protocols of mutual respect is never to cross your legs with your foot pointing toward your guest. Do not sit like a cowboy, she said. And do not touch their heads. I had rubbed many Viet kids' heads, I told her. That was all right, she said. But you are considered uncouth if you pat an elder on the back or rub his head.

Since arriving in this place I have gradually opened up to their culture. I know I don't belong, but I no longer feel alien around these people. Nothing they do, nothing they have to offer in my daily contact with them takes me aback.

Once Lan asked me after the class what "full of piss and vinegar" meant, pointing to an editorial in the *Stars and Stripes* that I had brought with me. "In Vietnam," I read, "the poor bastards had been at war for fifteen years. And here we come, full of piss and vinegar, wanting to win the war in six months." I explained that it meant "full of youthful energy," and she, not satisfied by the explanation, said, "Why can't they use some refined words instead of crude ones to express the same thing?" I wanted to tell her that my culture is unrefined, that the cowboy tongue usually gets the better of me before I can rephrase my thoughts. But it was too much to try to explain that to her, so I just laughed.

There is one thing, though, that I'll never get used to: The sight of their black-lacquered teeth. It shocked me the first time I saw one of their elders smile. It shocked most of our men, especially the West Pointers. Those with brilliant minds in physics and mathematics, who understand how the B-52's all-metal skin works, how the wrinkled appearance of the fuselage's forward section expands and becomes smooth when the aircraft gains altitude. Those who know Samuel Huntington's credo on how to defeat a people who are struggling against foreign intervention: "Dry up the ocean so that the fish don't have any water." What would these educated men think when they first met a Viet whose teeth were all black? But, Mamma, I understand these people. I eat their rice, rice that we burn so the Viet Cong can't feast on it, rice soiled with buffalo dung that they must bring home and sift through with care because rice is the staple of their livelihood, rice that grows in paddies where we kill the Viets sometimes indiscriminately and later the farmers bury the bodies and harvest the rice and by then the bloodstains on the rice stalks have turned the color of paddy dirt.

*

Dear Mamma,

The Viet Cong attacked our platoon outside the village. It was half past three in the morning. We held our position but when dawn broke we could hear gunfire in the village and we knew that the Viet Cong had punched through the village by holding us at bay long enough on the riverbank. At first light a pair of jetfighters showed up, dropping low, skimming the treetops still wet with dew. They spotted the Viet Cong in the long canal that flanks the village and flows into the Trem River, and released napalm bombs on them. From the river we saw flames and smoke and soon the wind brought with it the foul smell of petroleum. We could hear guns roar each time the jetfighters came swooping down, drawing enemy fire, and we could hear the trees burning and bamboo popping, and the air felt hot on our faces. The fumes reeked so bad we had to cover our noses with our hankies. The jet fighters repelled the attack and once the mist burned off, we moved into the village.

We came upon a long line of men and women frantically digging a trench between the side of the village and the canal. The wind was fanning the fire that licked the brush on the canal bank. People started cutting down cajeput trees to prevent the fire from spreading. I found Lan. I had prayed that I would see her again and when I saw her, spade in hand, dirt-smeared face hardened with pain, I crossed myself and took out my entrenching tool to join them. We chopped and hacked away climbing fern and tree roots, and the severed roots of milkwood trees dangled white and dripped sap like leaky faucets. We dumped dirt from the trench into the raging fire. The peat soil is so porous it was easy to dig and each stab of a spade brought the soil crashing down. An elder told Lan to dig quickly but not to swing her arms too high so she wouldn't tire out too soon and she passed the message on. The fire roared past the canal bank and the trees shivered and crackled. I could see the shimmering water, but knew why they didn't use it against the fire, for water only helps the napalm fire gain strength. Through the smoke I could see Lan's back. The heat grew, my lungs felt soaked with gasoline. The trench grew longer, deeper and wider until the fire came upon us and breathed a murderously hot air on our faces. Some slow-footed women and children got burned. People had to pull them away and as they pulled at the skin and the clothes with their hands, the jellied petroleum stuck to their skin and they and the victims all screamed in agony.

By evening the fire had stopped at the trench. The sky was a hazy yellow and the heat of the day and the heat of the fire had waned. Lan stood leaning on her spade, her face blackened from dirt and soot, her blouse stained with sweat. She gazed at the ruins and I took out my canteen and gave it to her. "Drink," I said. "Things will get back to normal." She took a sip, coughed and said, "This is the worst I have seen." Her voice was soft. Around her people stood contemplating the charred landscape, their eyes glassy, their figures darkening into silhouettes in the dusk. Along the bank Lan picked up a tortoise as it tried to crawl downwind away from the heat still simmering on the ground.

*

Dear Mamma,

It has taken over two months to rebuild the village. I helped as often as I could. I'll be going on a seven-day leave to Singapore tomorrow.

I gave Lan a gift; a paintbox and a notebook with handwritten poems. The paintbox was enameled white with two deep mixing wells. The notebook, pressed together by two pieces of faded brown cardboard, had drawings and poems written neatly in Vietnamese on the ruled-line sheets. She asked me where I got them from and I told her from a dead North Vietnamese soldier's rucksack. I couldn't throw the notebook away. Each page was illustrated with drawings of flowering twigs and solitary blossoms, of floating clouds and a full moon.

I knew it was a sad gift to give. The notebook no longer had an owner. It was like smelling a dead flower, but it moved her. "These are love poems," she said, "He was yearning for home and his sweetheart."

I asked her to show me. She put her finger under two words, "*Yêu em.*" Love you. I mouthed the words. Loud enough for her to hear.

*

Dear Mamma,

On my Recreation and Recuperation leave in Singapore, I bought myself a three-piece suit for fifty dollars and a long sapphire-blue silk scarf. I settled on the scarf because I didn't know what else Lan would like. She always wore indigo or sapphire blouses. I could imagine her wearing the scarf. I wrote the words "*Yêu em*" on the back of a card and put it in the giftwrapped box.

When I came back to the base camp, the cajeput was deep green, the river was white with water lilies along the edge of the riverbank, and the scent of the flowers was on the air. My platoon was still out in the bush. I told the others I was going to make my way to the Catholic village, but one of them took me aside and told me it was gone. He said the boys pulled out right after I left on my R&R and the following night the Viet Cong overwhelmed the village defense and walked every villager to the Trem River. They shot each of them in the head and kicked the bodies into the water. He said the river turned red. Those who hid away survived and were later taken to the New-Life Hamlet, a free-fire zone. I found out that less than twenty had made it to that place and Lan wasn't one of them.

I had to see the ruins for myself. Before I pull my two-hour guard duty, a buddy of mine drove me to the Catholic village. As I sat on the Jeep, bare-headed in the heat, something was gnawing at my stomach. It has been gnawing at me since I learned of the tragedy. When I left the ruins of the village and rode back on the 10-ton thunder truck mounted with a quad-50 machine gun, the truck went up along the Trem River. In the bright morning the deep green of cajeput was breathtaking, the river white with water lilies. I watched the river go by and couldn't make sense of what had happened. It did not add up as I thought of a home with her, watching the storks taking flight from the river, going, going until they reached their roosts in a cajput grove.

The American Prisoner

We stayed deep in the jungle. To reach us, it would take two full days on foot from the Mekong Delta. We hacked away brush and vines and bamboo thickets and leveled the fern-covered ground to build our camp. Above us rose giant trees, one rising above another so that they formed foliaged crowns so thick when it rained mere drops sluiced down the curves of the vault. When the sun reached its zenith at midday, it looked like twilight below.

The American prisoners were quartered in a thatched hut, low lying with three mud-and-bamboo laced sides. Its open side faced a guard shack outside the bamboo enclosure. I could see them moving around, drooped, heads bent. The hut was built that way so that, to move around, the prisoners had to lower their heads all the time. That adopted posture would eventually affect their psyches. Outside the fence, along its base where the earth was thick with creepers, a line of bamboo stakes was planted underground. None of the prisoners would try to escape, because the booby traps might not kill them but the wilderness beyond would.

*

He was one of the first American prisoners of war I saw. He could speak Vietnamese and, except in long statements, he had only a slight accent. I heard his prison mates call him Ian. Later I heard that he had been with us for six months. They captured him before his friends could get to him. They had to carry him. His legs were messed up from one of our handmade mines. A piece of metal from the mine was still lodged in his head. He said our doctors told him they couldn't remove it, not that they didn't want to try, but they didn't want to risk his life by doing so. He only slept on the side of his head opposite the wound. He said it gave him a numbing headache if he slept on the other side. It was his bad karma, he said, that he had stepped on the mine. He said it in Vietnamese and we all laughed at the word he used. *Nghiep*. Smart man. Said the mine was made from a howitzer shell. American artillery shell, he said. Then he winked at us as we sensed the irony.

When the mine went off, he screamed, then blacked out. Upon

waking, he felt like he'd been hit on the side of the head with a blackjack.
O death, where is your victory? O death, where is your sting? He said the Bible
words in his head. He saw faces looking down at him. Crowned by oyster-
colored pith helmets. He said—without even opening his mouth—*Làmon!*

*

He had a frail frame, his red-haired head always lolling to one side. I
said to him in English, "No one wants to die."

"To die is gain," he said. Then he quickly added, "That's from the
Bible. You Catholic?"

"No." I shook my head.

"Buddhist?"

"No."

"No religion?"

"None."

He eyed me, his lips puckered. He looked so gaunt, so malnourished,
his cheekbones cut sharp like Vietnamese cheekbones.

"I'm surprised they didn't kill you back there," I said.

"They didn't," he said, this time in Vietnamese. "But the people in
the next village almost did."

"What did they do?"

"This woman came running to me," he said. "She had a hoe in her
hands. I was in a litter. The guards didn't see her. I raised one arm to
avert the blow. I grabbed a guard by his shirt with my other arm. He
grabbed the hoe and shoved her back."

His words came out slowly. His Vietnamese accent was neutral,
neither northern nor southern. He must have picked up the language
from all sorts of speakers. He said short statements in Vietnamese, but
when he talked at length, he would throw in English words. Likewise,
I'd fall back on Vietnamese when I talked with him in English. And we
understood each other very well.

He paused to regain his breath. His eyes were serene. Hazel eyes.
They never darted while he spoke to you. Never a second thought
fleeting in them. I liked him.

He asked for a Vietnamese word. Cinders. Then another. Mortar.
He said, "I saw many huts burned to cinders on our way through. Half
the village was gone. People gathered along the dirt road. They pointed

toward me on the litter and yelled, *Meey! Meey!* I was the main attraction. We went past a graveyard. There were a number of fresh graves, I could tell by the color of fresh dirt. In front of a grave, I saw three mortar shells laid out in a row. Iron-rust color. They were duds."

He said the word "duds" in English. I said I knew what it meant. He said, "I'm sure they'll be used as booby traps on us. Then a guard spoke to me in his broken English, 'See that man?' I tried to follow his hand pointing toward the crowd. 'See that woman? That boy?' Then he pointed toward the fresh graves and kept nodding at me. I took that to mean that one of those fresh graves had been part of the woman's family."

*

Ian asked me for the word "blowfly." He remembered the *ruoi xanh*. The flies had been following him for three days. By then his legs began to smell. He could see white eggs in his wounds. "You pick them and leave them in the sun and they will hatch in three hours," he said. "I saw it myself." Some hatched in his wounds. They turned purplish blue. But he never let the wounds bother him. The pain throbbed, horribly at times. The smell had grown stronger. He tried to rise to salute the camp commander. A guard yelled at him. "Bow!" He steadied himself and lowered his head at the commander. Then he slumped to the cot. White maggots dropped from his wounds to the dirt floor. The commander winced. Later in the day a nurse came in. Before she did, a guard told him of her arrival. From what the guard said—"Americans number ten"—he gathered that she hated him and his kind. The girl was young. Clear-eyed, perky. Yet she wore a glum look about her as she poured alcohol on his legs. The wounds smarted. He felt ashamed when she pinched her nose, then donned a mask and worked on a pair of surgical gloves. As she squeezed the pus out of the wounds, he looked down at her gentle face. He held still, not even breathing, while she swabbed the wounds with a cotton-tipped hemostat. He watched her bandage his wounds deftly, neatly, and he could smell the fresh gauze, the stinging antiseptic. As she handed him a small bottle of antibiotic, he said in English, "What's your name, Miss?" She looked into his eyes in silence. No English, he thought, and then tried to put together a couple of Vietnamese words. She looked at his bandaged head. "Do you have much headache?" she said in English. "Yes," he said. "I can't sleep." She motioned for him to sit up and then unwrapped the gauze and checked the gash. She changed the gauze. "Our doctor will look at this," she said. He felt comforted by her soft voice. She turned to leave and he called to her, "You didn't tell me your name, Miss." She answered without turning her head, "You don't need to know."

A few days after the young nurse cleaned and wrapped his leg wounds, Ian had a fever. The pain returned to his legs. He ate very little from his meager meals and lay the rest of the day shivering on the rickety cot. He couldn't walk, so every day an interrogator came to his cot. The interrogator spoke hardly any English and was accompanied by an interpreter. Ian told them what he knew. He'd thought about the interrogation before they came. He knew he must tell whatever they asked, not to lie but at the same time not to risk the lives of his fellow soldiers with what he told them. He'd memorized the Code of Conduct. He also knew how much he should say under the Geneva Convention for the treatment of the prisoners of war. But all that vanished when the interrogator said, "You are a criminal of war and you will be treated accordingly." At that, Ian gave them only his name, rank, and date of birth. When pressed, he gave them his service number and unit. He kept silent on the military questions. The interrogator glanced at Ian's legs and gave them a quick tap with his metal ruler. He mouthed his words in Vietnamese and when he stopped, the interpreter said, "We will treat your legs if you cooperate. If you do not, you will eventually lose your legs to amputation because of unavoidable abscesses." Ian said, "I will tell you what I know. Radio frequency? No, I am not a radioman. How many M-79s in the company? No, I am a rifleman, I only know what's in my squad. Other weapons carried by the company? No, I am in a rifle squad, my knowledge of weapons is limited to my squad." The interrogator asked, "How did you get to Vietnam?" Surprised, Ian said nothing. It must be a trick question. At the interrogator's silence, he said, "By airplane. Twenty hours by airplane." The interrogator turned to the interpreter. "*Hai muoi gio à?*" The interpreter nodded. Twenty hours. The interrogator said, "*Ôi!*" His baffled exclamation had Ian nodding to confirm what he'd just said. "Very far," Ian said. They both shook their heads in bewilderment. "Give us your family's address in America," the interrogator said. Ian felt perplexed. "What for?" he asked. "Just give," the interrogator said. Ian heard in his head the ugly threat about his legs. He thought of the distance between shores. He told them his family's address. Unsettled, he felt cross. The interrogator said something incomprehensible in English. The interpreter then said to Ian, "What is your father's profession?" Ian studied the men, then said, "He is dead." "What was his profession when he was alive?" "He was a . . . civilian," Ian said. "Who did he work for?" "He was a car mechanic." The interrogator winced and asked the interpreter, who asked Ian, "He repair automobiles?" Ian nodded. The interrogator mused, then said something to the interpreter, who asked, "Where did he die?" "At home." "What did he die of?" Ian looked down at the floor. "Cirrhosis of the liver," he admitted. "What?" the interrogator asked. "He died of sickness," Ian said. But the interrogation went on for two more days until the interrogator felt satisfied with the consistency of Ian's answers. By then, biting down the pain in his legs, Ian began to grit his teeth. But only momentarily. Evil pain. Horrible pain. He knew now why people killed themselves when pain became unbearable. Then a doctor came. The doctor felt his calves, probing with his fingers. Each probe made Ian swallow his moans. The doctor shot his legs with novocaine and proceeded to clean out the wounds with a hemostat, the way the nurse did. Then he picked the metal splinters out of the wounds. It took a long time. After the last sliver was removed, he shot Ian's legs with penicillin. His thick glasses fogged when he was done bandaging Ian's legs. He clapped shut his medical satchel. "You are gud," he said. "Tomorrow I give you more penicillin and I luk at your head."

*

There came more American prisoners now, a dozen more, since I saw him that first time. By now Ian's legs had healed but his head wound still gave him a constant headache. He'd never smoked before he had the headache. Now he chain-smoked. He knew how to roll cigarettes like us, his captors. Thumbs, middle fingers twirling and coaxing the tobacco-packed paper into a tight, stubby cylinder, the paper edge quickly licked to seal it. He took a drag, sitting on his haunches just like a Vietnamese, his arms flopping over his knees, the cigarette hanging between his lips the way Vietnamese smoked their hand-rolled joints. On a nearby cot sat a blond American, thin as a reed, with the hairiest eyebrows like caterpillars, who shook his head at Ian. "Doesn't he look like a gook, eh?" Some of the prisoners had begun to squat like gooks. They also rolled up their trouser legs past their knees like gooks. From their cigarette ration that he had pooled together, Ian bribed a guard with two dozen cigarettes in exchange for a small bottle of *Nhi Thiên Duong*, the pungent, comfort-soothing eucalyptus oil the Vietnamese would daub on their nostrils and temples when sick. Squatting on his heels, Ian smeared his palm with a streak of the blue-gum oil and then rolled his cigarette back and forth over the streak. He passed the bottle to a next guy among the smokers. "Conserve it," he said. "That's precious as gold." He lit his cigarette, sucked on it deeply and closed his eyes. The acrid smell of hand-rolled cigarettes momentarily distracted them from the rotten odor in the hut. It wasn't from the kitchen—an aperture in the ground lined with rocks with a long bamboo tube that carried the cooking smoke and dispersed it out of sight of the American spotter planes. The odor came from outside, ten feet away in the rear of the hut, where the open-air latrine was—a hole in the ground covered with a wooden plank. Blowflies would drop eggs in the hole whenever someone forgot to lid it, and soon the pit was alive with maggots and the air was humming with metallic blue, green flies. Sometimes a hen or rooster would come and stick its head in the hole to peck away the maggots among the muck. When I came by his hut I'd stay outside, for a permanent stench pervaded it when the breeze blew and on a hot day the god-awful smell would give everyone a headache.

*

It rained all night. In the morning the distant mountain lay shrouded in a fog burning slowly off as another wall of fog would come rolling in, thinned by the sun and drifting away like a hallucination.

Outside the prisoners' hut I saw Ian sitting on his haunches, swathed in a burlap bag. It was what we gave the prisoners for a blanket. We took the US Agency for International Development rice bags—stamped on the outside with a clasped-hands logo above the line *Donated by the People of the United States of America*—cut them open and sewed them together to the size of a small blanket. It was chilly. Ian peered up at me, his hands palming a tin cup. It must have been hot tea, for steam was curling up from the cup. They received a tea ration but never coffee, and by now most of them had probably forgotten what coffee tasted like.

I drew deeply on my cigarette, and his gaze followed my hand motion as I exhaled a plume of smoke. I could tell he craved a cigarette. Yet I couldn't offer him one, because the guard in the lookout shack behind me was probably watching. "Tea is good on a morning like this," I said to him in English.

"This isn't tea," he said, dropping his gaze to the cup. "*Sua ngot.*"

He extended the cup. The condensed milk looked like chalk water. He sipped, holding it in his mouth as if to savor something precious. As he swallowed, he sucked in his cheeks. Gaunt and anemic looking, his face had a fuzzy line along the jaw. His beard wasn't growing anymore, his red hair was thinning out because of malnutrition. He clasped his hands around the cup, shivering.

"Where are your sandals?" I asked, looking down at his bare feet. Hunched up, with the burlap bag draping his back, he looked like a pelican at rest.

"Saving them," he said, eyeing my black-rubber sandals. "Wearing them only when I go picking greens."

They would go with the guards deeper in the forest to pick wild greens and the guards would tell them which plants they should avoid if they wanted to live another day—most of the greens were inedible and some poisonous. Often, they brought back wild banana flowers and then peeled away the tough outer layers until they reached the tender-looking, finger-length buds, yellow and lithe. They would cook them in watered-down *nuoc mam* and eat them with cooked rice. They craved fish sauce, which was rationed, so Ian told me they added water to the fish sauce and boiled it. The heated *nuoc mam* would taste much saltier that way.

Sipping his watered-down milk, he told me they received a can of condensed milk the other day to share among themselves. Each one got a spoonful to add to his cup of hot water and the diluted milk was so thin it barely tasted sweet anymore. He said the trick was to drink it hot to intensify the sweetness. He said he hoped to receive another can of condensed milk soon, because fresh supplies had just arrived. At my quizzical look, he grinned and pointed toward the trail beyond the lookout shack and said he saw women carrying USAID burlap bags into camp the prior evening. I nodded, remembering one time he asked me why the women porters had large banana fronds covering their backs beneath the bags, and I explained to him that the fronds helped keep their sweat from soaking into the rice bags. "Ingenious," he said. "Just common sense," I said. He shook his head. "No, I mean the way they took our AID bags and turned them into backpacks with straps sewn on them for carrying things."

Like most prisoners, he cherished rice. Between rice and boiled manioc, they would beg for rice and *nuoc mam*, which they treasured for the scarcity of salt. Once, I saw him sitting outside under the sun with the rice pot between his knees. "Rat shit," he said. I could see black clumps among the shiny rice grains. Whenever they forgot to lid their rice pot, as they would with their latrine, rats would get in the pot in the night and eat the grains. Mornings they would have to wash the rice grains to get rid of rat feces which, at times, were so clumped up with the grains they could not be separated.

The next day I gave Ian a handful of black seeds and told him to soak them in water overnight and then plant them. "*Mong toi*," I told him. "Red-stem spinach. Very nutritious."

The following day I saw him behind the hut, burying seeds in the soil. "Some kind of seeds," he said to me and showed me the can in which he'd soaked them. The color of the water was wine-red. I explained to him that the red-stem spinach would grow as tall as an average Viet man and he said, "I'll build a teepee for it."

"What's a teepee?" I asked.

"Wait till you see it," he said and started splitting bamboo. He drove the strips into the ground and tied the splits with the *choai* strings—the vines from a swamp fern plant that we would soak in water and use as ropes. The conical-shaped support he built became a home for the climbing spinach. Monsoon rains that soaked the forest for days helped the seeds sprout quickly. In two weeks, scarlet stems began pushing up and twining around the teepee, and pale green leaves shot out from the stems that now lost their baby red and turned into a deep-wine red. After I showed him how to cook the spinach, he went around collecting more than two dozen cigarettes and traded them with the guards for two chicken eggs. He cooked the spinach in the two pots they had—the rice pot and the pot for boiling water—and borrowed from the guards another pot to cook their rice. He had his mates crush a handful of red peppers that they grew behind their hut and mixed them with the diluted *nuoc mam* in a wooden bowl. He cut up the two boiled eggs and dropped them into the bowl. It was the first time I saw the prisoners eat together, sitting on their haunches in a circle, the pots in the center on the dirt floor, arms flying, chopsticks clacking, shoveling rice into their mouths, dipping clumps of spinach into the egg-and-red-pepper *nuoc mam*, inhaling their food and all forgetting the latrine-nauseating stink that made the air blister.

*

Summer drew to a close and that year the cicadas hung on stubbornly in the trees. You could hear them ringing and shrilling across the air, deep in the tangles of cajeput and bamboo groves. Ian and his mates had seen the guards hunt baby cicadas at night, and the sight of flickering lanterns around the bases of trees had become familiar around the camp. They looked for newly hatched cicadas. The cicadas peeked through the earth, crawled up tree trunks, and shed their skins. Their wings were pale. Before the nymphs' new skins could harden—their wings would fill with fluid to turn themselves into adults—the guards would pick them, one by one off the tree trunks. They would drop those nymphs into a salt-water pot, so the nymphs' wings would stop stiffening, and then they would boil them. In a wok they stir-fried them with granulated salt, and you could smell a mouth-watering aroma coming out of the camp kitchen.

At noon when I walked by the prisoners' hut, I heard Ian call out from inside: "Giang!" He was sitting on the dirt floor with five of his mates, the lidded rice pot on the floor among them. Inside the hut the terrible smell from the latrine made me hold my breath. I saw what they had cooked for lunch. To go with their rice, they had boiled corn, which they grated and doused with *nuoc mam* mixed with crushed hot peppers. "You want *ve*?" Ian asked me, holding the rice bowl in midair.

"*Ve*?" I said. "Cicada?"

He nodded, shushing me with a finger to his lips. I looked toward the guard's hut and turned back. "You caught the baby cicadas," I said, curious. The prisoners were forbidden to go outside their hut at night, except to use the latrine in the full view of the guard. One of his mates lifted the lid on the rice pot and inside, piled up above the cooked rice, were stir-fried baby cicadas. Ian picked one up. "Try it," he said. The cicada had a smoky smell when I sank my teeth into it. It popped with a *plup* sound. A fatty flavor rich with raw salt bit my tongue. "This is good," I said to him, licking my lips, feeling all my taste buds rise up. "You caught them?"

"Late last night," he said. Popping sounds came from the rice pot and the lid was quickly put back on. They all grinned happily, like children on the Lunar New Year.

*

We had a late-summer storm. Most of the roofs suffered damage and we had a shortage of drinking water. The storm and heavy rains had roiled the creek nearby, from which we ran a long bamboo channel to our kitchen and from the kitchen the prisoners were to carry water to their own hut in hard-rubber containers. Mud was everywhere. Red mud left footprints on the dirt floors, the footpaths, on cots and hammocks.

For days the rain came and went. During the lulls the heat beat down on the forest and the forest floor steamed. While we lay the footpaths with wooden planks, the prisoners were taken to a distant grassland to cut buffalo grass and elephant grass, bundle them and carry them back to camp to thatch the roofs. I saw them hauling back large bundles of it. It was a sweltering day and the forest vapors hazed the air. I saw Ian sit down on his heels by the trail to take a breather. He was naked to the waist, his back striped with cuts from grass blades. They smarted with their toothy blades, and their coarse undersides caused skin rash. You would scratch yourself until your skin chafed. The guards ordered him to move on, and I could see the heat was taking its toll on him. His legs looked rubbery, his head hung to one side.

We worked long days into nights until our camp was restored. At night it turned cold. I had to put on another shirt and, wrapped tightly in my blanket, I still shivered. I thought of the prisoners and their burlap blankets. Each of them had only one shirt and one pair of pants. I had seen them join their cots so they could draw heat from each other, each sleeping balled up in the fetal position to keep warm. A few days later Ian came down with dysentery. They said he had drunk unboiled water that the prisoners carried back to their hut from our kitchen, unclean water from the nearby creek. I understood that the prisoners had neglected boiling their own drinking water because they were taken every day to the grassland to cut buffalo grass, a long trek. From dehydration to bone-chilling cold at night, something had to give. Some prisoners suffered diarrhea. One of them walked around with no pants in the hut. The guards told him to put his pants back on and the next thing they saw was watery discharge running down his legs. I went into the hut to check on Ian a few times and he wasn't doing well. He could hardly sit because his testicles had swollen to the size of a tomato. His legs and his stomach puffed grotesquely. At night sometimes the urge to release was so sudden and great, he would let it gush out of his body onto his cot. The guards would make them clean the floor every day to get rid of the excrement.

*

Within days summer was over. One morning we heard the sound of airplanes and the next day too, then several days after. The droning of the planes soon became familiar in the early days of that autumn. Nobody knew what the lumbering planes were doing, except that everyone would feel like they had just walked out into a drizzle and felt a dampness on their faces. Everywhere it was damp. The thatch roofs were wet, the hammocks were wet, and leaves began to fall, suddenly browned and withered—not the brown or red of autumnal leaves—and the grass yellowed like in drought. Then we learned about those C-123 planes and the chemicals they sprayed on the forest. The spray fell like mist, wetting the leaves, and the air smelled tart. On the morning we woke and saw a giant canopy of the forest cleared away; the mountain showed through as if the forest had moved overnight toward it. On that day Ian's red-stem spinach died.

That afternoon I visited Ian in his hut. I brought him a can of condensed milk. He looked so pale and his face so misshapen that he shocked me with his smile. "*Cám on,*" he said, holding the can tightly in his hand.

"You are welcome," I said, standing by his cot and holding my breath. His teeth were clattering. I took out a Gauloises Caporals cigarette pack and placed it in his other hand.

"This-thing-is-strong," he said, slurring.

"Help me cut down," I said with a grin.

He held up the blue-colored pack, gazing at the winged helmet logo, while I let out my breath slowly. I could see dark blotches on the fly of his pants and on the inside of his pants legs. The legs had swollen noticeably.

"Our treasure plant died," he said, raising his voice with an effort.

"The spinach in the back?"

He nodded.

I told him about the chemicals the two-engine Caribous had sprayed on our forest. He said nothing for a while, then, "So they can see you. That's bad."

"Bad for all of us," I said, thinking of him and his sick mates if we had to move.

That evening, after supper, Ian lapsed into a coma and died before midnight. They said he craved sweet so he drank half the can of condensed milk without eating his evening meal. Our doctor said that so much condensed milk could be fatal for a dysentery victim. In the morning we gave them a coffin to bury Ian, and his mates carried the coffin to the camp's graveyard and dug a grave. They were digging when we heard the plane and soon we saw a spotter coming over the forest. The prisoners stopped and lowered the casket. It was a shallow grave. They said the Lord's Prayer in the droning of the plane as it disappeared over the mountain.

Sometime in the afternoon the sky buzzed and throbbed with the sounds of helicopters. The gongs alerted us to aerial attack and many of us, including the prisoners, were forced into the bomb shelters. From underground we heard the gunships firing rockets and the roaring of their miniguns and we heard our antiaircraft in concealed locations around the camp. The tremors went through the earth and we could feel it shake in our bunkers.

It was dusk when we left the bomb shelters. Most of the huts were destroyed, our kitchen and the prisoners' hut too. The graveyard was hit with rockets and large holes in the ground gaped. We could see old coffins upheaved, many burst open, flung about. We could see the fresh graves gutted and there wasn't anything left in them.

It was sultry. As I walked away from the graveyard in the hooting of owls, something clawed at my throat. I'd once told Ian I had no religion. Had I faith, what solace could it give me now?

The charred smell was in the air and followed me through the forest, and I kept walking in the pitch dark until I saw more bomb craters. I stood over the rim of a crater, looking down into the black pit, until my body and my head went numb.

The Virgin's Mole

I watch her from the window of my room. The morning heat comes early. In her cut-off jeans with white frays at the thighs, Chi Lan leans against the doorjamb, legs crossed at the knees, gazing at the old man in the back lot with the bone in his hand. She swats at a mosquito, arm cocked, smooth and white in her cerise sleeveless blouse.

The old man is tapping down the soil in a fresh hole he's dug under the lemon tree. With the window shutters open, I can smell the rusty heat. I draw deeply on my cigarette and cough until my eyes water. When I look up I see her outside the open window looking in.

"Hello, *chú*!" she says, smiling. Her voice is soft with a lilt in *chú*. *Uncle.*

I cover my mouth with my hand and nod at her.

"Are you all right?" she asks, leaning in on her folded arms on the windowsill.

"Yeah. How are you?"

"Fine." The word barely leaves her lips when she drops her gaze to the folding table. Atop it is a stack of paper, a cigarette pack, and a Zippo lighter as its paperweights. A black pencil lies across an ashtray. On the top sheet, a pencil sketch. She tilts her head, looking at the sketch. "You draw, *chú*?"

"Yeah." I mash my cigarette in the ashtray.

"May I see them?"

"Do you draw, too, Chi Lan?"

"No," she says, laughing. I pass her the stack of papers through the window. She sweeps her hair back over her ear. Her lower lip tucked in, she seems to blend into the sketch I've made. She has a tiny black mole under the corner of her left eye. She blinks when she sees me looking at her.

"Is this a battlefield?" she asks, pointing to a boot in the drawing.

"What makes you say that?"

"This military boot," she says. "The smoke, and the burned down trees."

"Okay."

"Okay what?"

"A battlefield."

"Whose boot is it?"

"An American GI's boot."

Her eyes return to the sketch. Black, white, gray. The fire-consumed peat turned in its top layer to gray. Tree stumps, fallen limbs in charred black, bare roots like wildly flung arms entwined in black and gray. Wisps of smoke hovering over the ground.

"Are they ghosts?" she asks, tracing her finger on the eddies of smoke.

"Just smoke."

"They have human shapes," she says. "Our eyes trick us sometimes, though. And what do you call this, this rooster in Vietnamese? Is it a jungle cock?"

The fowl stands with its combed, wattled head erect between a smoking tree stump and the boot. "Ga rung," I say, looking up at her.

She repeats the words, slightly accented. She has lived in America for a long time. "Where was this battlefield?"

"From my memory."

"From a real place?"

"Does it matter?"

I shrug. If she knew this land as well as I do, she would recognize the peat ground that only exists here in the U Minh region.

"You were in it, right?"

"I was in many battles. They're all pieces of recollection now."

"My mother said many war veterans don't want to remember their pasts."

She starts to turn over one sheet after another. Sketches of people, of things. Remembered. Unremembered. That's how you unburden your memories.

"Oh!" the girl exclaims. "You have him in here, too?"

I look at the sketch I did of the old man, on his haunches in his bone-burying routine. She knows about his ritual now because I have told her. She was as shocked as I was the first time seeing him at it.

He and his wife had a son who served in the Army of the Republic of Vietnam. One morning I looked out the window to see the old man digging near a starfruit tree, a small figure clad in white pajamas and a black trilby on his head.

After digging down a foot or so, he stopped. From the pocket of his pajamas he pulled out a bone. It looked like a wrist bone. He sat on his haunches and placed the bone in the hole and scooped dirt over it. After a while, the old woman came out, grabbed him by the arm, and dragged him inside. The next morning he was out there digging again. The same spot. I could hear the sound of his spade hitting the bone and saw him stop. He picked up the bone, smeared with brown dirt, and dragged his spade to the lemon tree. He fretted about the placement of the bone, turning it this and that way.

I had to ask the old woman. She told me that their son was killed in action somewhere in IV Corps in 1967. Exactly twenty years ago. They never found his body.

"You draw beautifully," Chi Lan says to me.

Then she stops turning the sheets, her gaze fixed on a sketch.

"You drew me?"

"That's not you."

"I'm sorry." She studies the face in the drawing. The only difference between her and the girl in the drawing is the long plait of hair. Knotted toward the end with a ribbon, flung over a shoulder.

"I never braid my hair like that," she says. "Maybe I will when I grow my hair that long."

"You've never had it that long?"

She shakes her head. "Who is she then?"

"Someone from memory."

"Of course," Chi Lan says. "I mean, who is she to you?"

"Someone I knew when I was your age. Or maybe I was younger."

*

Chi Lan leans on the windowsill, watching me place the slow drip coffee filter on a cup. The stainless-steel filter looks like a square-topped hat, the luster of morning light in its metal.

"You must wake early," she says. "I smell coffee around four. The owners don't drink coffee, so it must be you."

Her room is above mine. For fresh air, the windows are open day and night.

"Does it wake you?" I ask.

"I like the smell. I usually fall back to sleep. Then my mother gets up and leaves."

The local guide would arrive shortly after sunrise and drive her mother to the river where they will go to the forest in his motorboat.

"Join me for a cup of coffee then, when you're finally up."

"You drink it black, *chú?*"

"Always."

"I can never get used to black coffee."

She leaves the window, comes to the table. The coffee aroma begins to rise.

I tell her to sit on my bed, not on my rickety chair. I have fixed all the wobbly chairs in the inn except mine. She asks when I'll get mine fixed too, and I say that when I go to town the next time to get a haircut I will buy some parts for the chair.

She cups her feet with her hands. Her toenails are painted rose. I can see she wants me to notice them.

"You painted them last night?" I ask.

"You're very observant."

I shift my weight, and the chair creaks.

"Your hair is awfully long," she says. "Are you going to town soon, *chú?*"

"Yeah. And I won't forget the chair."

"It creaks like a mouse. Doesn't it annoy you?"

"No. It's just an old chair."

"Everything is old in this place. Old and so slow."

"We live a slow life here. I'm sure you'll forget everything by the time you go back home."

"I keep the things I learn—things I select to remember."

"Like what?" I say.

She shrugs. "Like the drip coffee. I'll remember that. And I'm fascinated with the rivers and canals around here. And the lives that depend on them."

She must have meant the floating market on Ông Doc River that runs through our town. I took her there just last week. We stood on a bridge looking down as the sun was rising and the river shone white in the mist that hung like a translucent mosquito net over the sampans. The sleepy river woke at the first sounds of oars as skiffs thin as a leaf glided to and fro, bringing the first customers to the market. We could see rows of boats and sampans moored along the riverbank, and the water was silvery in the morning sun. Nobody knows, I told her, how and when the floating market had come into being. Perhaps when some sampans came to rest along the sleepy bank, the oarswomen asked each other for a light, maybe a betel chew, a bottle gourd, a pumpkin, or a dash of *nuoc mam*—fish sauce. And, after a while, a little flea market took to life and then one day a floating market was born.

She took many photographs during her first trip to the forest with her mother. I was their local guide then. Her young mind spotted so many things that I could never think of her as a Vietnamese.

"Do you feel like a foreigner to your own birthplace?" I ask.

"I don't feel foreign to Vietnam. I remember the place where I came from. It looks just like the places around here."

"Where? You've never told me."

"You never asked."

"Where then?"

"Plain of Reeds. In the Mekong Delta, too."

"I know where it is. What do you remember?"

"The floods that came every year after summer. The canals that took you to the big rivers. The mangrove trees in the Plain. The stilt houses along the rivers." She crosses her legs, her finger tracing the sewn-on rose on her cutoffs. Her eyes are distant, though she is looking straight at me. "Do you remember those empty stilts along the riverbank? Just stilts on the mud bank with no houses on them?"

"What about them?"

"The other day, I photographed them. But I thought, what happened to the houses they supported? Stilts, but no houses. I used to see them when I went to the riverbank with the nuns. I grew up in an orphanage in the Plain of Reeds. The nuns ran it."

She pauses, glances down at the filter-covered coffee cup. "Is it ready?"

I lift the lid. The coffee has pooled, black and glossy, filling half the cup. She inhales. I pour a dash of black coffee into a fresh cup and add some hot water. She palms the cup with both hands, head lowered, the cup raised to her lips. She takes the first sip gingerly, her brow furrowed.

"Bitter," she says.

"Like medicine?"

"Better than medicine," she says. "Do you know why?"

"Because it's coffee, *phin* coffee?"

"Because your mind tells you so. The aroma tells you so."

"How old were you at that time?"

"Barely five."

Chi Lan has serene eyes, elongated, dark, and pretty. She is getting used to the bitter taste of the *phin* coffee. This orphan child, having been displaced to grow up into a beautiful girl, is now trying to greet her homeland.

                                *

The next day the heat comes early, and by sunrise I have to open the shutters in my room.

Before the sun is high and the heat becomes truly unbearable, I pick up a machete and begin clearing the bushes along the front base of the veranda. In the bushes I find some old moss-covered logs still damp from yesterday's rain and ax them to small chunks so the snakes will have no place to nest. In fact, with the bushes uncovered, I can see the rocks have been worn slick by the snakes coming and going. Under one bush I find a small carton of seeds. It dawns on me that they are watercress seeds the old woman has asked me to sow. The summer heat is so thick now the seeds would sprout in a week. She had told me to plant them in the back next to the lemon tree where the old man buries and re-buries his ox bone. The last time he did that he unearthed all our freshly planted seeds of mustard greens. I had to erect a wire-mesh fence around the plot. I must keep an eye on him always.

I pick up the carton and empty the four tin cups that are half-filled with vinegar. We have many cartons of vegetable seeds we plant year-round, and I fit each carton's bottom with four wooden pegs. Each peg rests on a vinegar-filled cup. Without such protection, ants would devour the seeds. Before I came up with this solution, the old woman had told me about the constant disappearing seeds. She said once she saw a patch of watercress sprouting up in the land in the back, as though someone had sown the seeds there. I told her the ants did that. They eat the seed caps, which have nutrition they need, and leave the seeds behind. The seeds later sprout where the ants have left them.

I had left the carton behind the bush when Chi Lan and her mother arrived, and remind myself to plant the seeds today before the old woman asks again. She says most of our guests like watercress among their greens. After leaving the carton on the rear veranda, I go around the inn and empty all the receptacles of standing rainwater. I'd forgotten to turn those planters and flower pots upside down, and now several of them are filled with rainwater, becoming a breeding ground for mosquitoes. After dark, those whiners will come out. They can't fly far, but they breed and multiply wherever they find water.

Everyone else is still in bed. It's quiet in the rear of the inn. The air stands still as I go about sowing the watercress seeds. With this heat, I believe, we could be eating watercress in the next couple of days. When I stop to wipe my face I see a lone stork flying across the hazy sky. I can see its trailing pink legs and the black stripes underneath its wings. On the skunk tree a yellow weaver is coming back with blades of grass in its beak. The agave at the base of the tree is flowering for the first time. Its strong, broad and fleshy leaves are spiny along their edges. It must have flowered overnight. The flowers are bursting forth in busy bottle brushes, and their sunset red strikes the eye against the cactus-green of their leaves. When Chi Lan first saw the agave by the skunk tree, she thought it was cactus. I told her the old woman had wanted it uprooted so she could use the area for a vegetable plot, but to do this you'd need an ox to pull it up. Chi Lan smiled and said she liked its lone and fierce look. I said to her it looks unusual, but it's pretty when it flowers.

And she said, "I'll photograph it when it does."

*

I go into town to shop during a downpour. Around noon the rain begins slacking off. The sky is clearing and the breeze carries the heat south, leaving a breath of moistness in the air.

After putting the groceries away, I check on the old man and see that his wife is bathing him in the bathhouse adjoined to the side of the inn. Upstairs the door of Chi Lan's room is open, but I do not see her, so I go back down the stairs and out to the rear. The field blazes in the sun. Hazy wisps of vapor curl all over the ground. Then I see a sudden glint of beaded water on the agave bush as well as a dark shape beside it.

I run down the veranda to the rain-soaked field and find Chi Lan lying on her back next to the agave. She is drenched. Her leaf-green T-shirt clings to her skin and her hair is matted in strands all over her face. Slung across her shoulder is the camera strap, the camera itself in the crook of her arm. I grab her arm and check for a pulse. Her eyes are shut, lips parted slightly. I can feel her pulse. There are mud stains on the sides of her shorts, and her legs fold into each other at the knees as though she's sleeping. But no bite marks on her legs, which would have told of snakebite. Nothing on her neck either. Then I see a small red bump on her upper arm, near the elbow. The red looks fresh on her skin. I see the stinger. A wasp sting. The old woman got stung once by a wasp and fainted even after she had made it into the house. I pinch the end of the stinger with my long fingernails. The hard stinger comes out like a fishbone.

I gather Chi Lan in my arms and carry her up the veranda and into my room. She must be allergic to the wasp. I lay her on my bed and work the camera strap off her neck. The water is dripping from her clothes. The purplish color of her lips makes me wonder how long she has lain in the rain. I know I must do something. I snatch a bath towel from the wall hook, and, after some hesitation, begin drying her. Her skin is cold and her T-shirt is sopping wet. I manage to peel the T-shirt off her body. It drips onto the floor as I drape it over the back of the chair. I pull out a clean shirt in my old mango-wood dresser and, sitting down on the edge of the bed, I look at her. Her face is pale against her black hair. Then I look at her nakedness and hold my breath. She is so beautiful. I dry her hair, her face, her chest. The bright red mole on her bosom. I struggle to get my shirt on her, as if changing the shirt on a child. The shirt sags at her shoulders. I want her to wake. Her breathing comes heavier now.

I boil water on the hot plate and while waiting for the water to heat up, I cut some ginger slices and drop them into my coffee mug together with a tea bag. Chi Lan begins to stir. When I glance over, she is trying to sit up.

"*Chú,*" she says with some difficulty.

"Lie back," I say, moving to the bed.

She looks down at herself and touches her face then her arm, her eyes unfocused. "What happened?"

"You were stung by a wasp." I take out a cigarette. "Were you out there photographing something?"

"Yes, *chú*. The agave flowers." She looks at my cigarette. "Your cigarette is wet."

"From carrying you in."

"It won't even light."

"Maybe it won't." I tear the cigarette paper, set it on the bed and point at the brown tobacco. "I'm going to put this on the sting."

I hold her arm by the elbow, feeling her faint breathing against my forehead, and squint at the reddened bump.

"Is it venomous?" she asks, drawing a sharp breath.

"Nothing fatal. But it can knock you out." I daub a pinch of tobacco with my saliva and paste it on the lump. "Does it hurt?"

"It's stinging now." She bites her lower lip, rubbing the swelling. "You said a wasp did this?"

"Could be a digger wasp or a great black wasp. I've seen those around the inn."

After I bandage her arm, she pulls up her soiled legs and rests the bandaged arm on her knee. She massages the swelling. "I don't remember anything." She leans to one side, her eyelids fluttering. "Well, maybe I do. I felt something very painful on my arm. I took a few more pictures then suddenly felt dizzy."

"It'll take a day or so before the pain goes away."

The water boils. I pour hot water into the mug. Blowing on it, I bring it to her. "This will ease the sting."

She looks down, not taking the mug from me. "I'm wearing your shirt, *chú*."

"Yeah." I keep my voice even. "You were soaked through. I was worried. Have a sip of tea."

She says nothing, keeping her head down. The mug breathes curling vapor. She lifts the mug with both hands but avoids meeting my eyes. Her face reddens, but she hides her expression behind the mug with only her eyes visible. She glances at her T-shirt still dripping over the back of the chair. The tiny black mole dots the corner of her left eye, and I can't help but think of the red mole. My gaze makes her drop her head. She shifts. The bed creaks. Its white sheet is wet and stained black.

"Your bed is messed up," she says.

I nod just as she winces and touches the bandaged bite. Her mussed-up hair, still wet, gives her an untamed look, so pale, so raw.

"I'm surprised," she says with the mug still covering her face, "you could carry me in from out there."

"I had to. You're as light as air."

She watches me wipe her camera dry with the towel. "Thank you, *chú*," she says, caressing her bandaged forearm. "Are you sure it'll take the sting out of me, this tobacco paste?"

"I've done that myself. For wasp sting."

"You got stung by a wasp?"

"It knocked me out, like it did to you. We're both allergic to their sting."

She gives a small laugh. "I'd be dead now if it were a poisonous snake."

"So be careful when you're out there."

"I remember that you told me your father died from a snakebite. But he was a snake catcher." She offers me her mug of tea. "Would you like some of this?"

"Just one sip." I receive the mug from her, cupping my hands over hers.

"Didn't your father know how to doctor himself against snakebite?"

She sets the mug back on her knee.

"He could have. With an antidote." My gaze falls on the black mole by her eye. "Did you know that they make antidote for snake venom out of the venom itself? My father used to sell the venom he extracted from snakes to the professional snake catchers. I used to watch him squeeze a snake at the throat so hard the snake's mouth opened wide enough to jam in a cup. You should have seen how the snake's fangs hooked inside, and when he raked them the venom started oozing into the cup."

"Ew." She shivers. "What color?"

"Yellow." I look down at her mug. "Like that."

"Stop that." She giggles, then draws up her shoulders. "I wouldn't drink it now that I know."

"You can drink snake venom. It's harmless."

"No way, *chú*."

"My father used to mix it with rice liquor and drank it in one gulp. Said it's good for digestion."

"I thought it's deadly."

"If the snake bites you, yeah. Because its venom goes into your bloodstream. But not when you take it by the mouth."

"Why the difference?"

"By the mouth? The venom goes down to your stomach. The acid there will neutralize it." I pause, then add with a grin. "Where it's good for the digestion."

"Yes. But not for me."

She brushes strands of wet hair over her ears with her fingertips. The inky-black eyebrows that arch gracefully, the melodious voice. Her foot shifts and touches my hand. In the silence I can feel her tense.

"Why didn't your father protect himself with an antidote?" she asks.

"He was careless."

"And you were too young to tell him otherwise?"

"It made no difference. He used to tell me, 'Son, if a snake bites you on a finger and you've got no antidote around, chop off the finger. If it's a toe, chop off the toe. Then you'll live.' Easy to say. I'd seen men do that in the jungle during the war. Men with missing fingers and toes. My father had a jar of antidote we kept in the shack. But my father never carried it with him. Like he had a death wish. Or just careless."

She sips, listening. "One night," I say, "my father saw a girl sleeping outside our shack under the weeping fig. The base of that huge tree was a snake colony. With snakes crawling around in the bushes around the tree, my father thought she must have been dead. But she had passed out from hunger. This beggar girl was in her early twenties. So my father fed her a bowl of snake meat and some rice and let her sleep on the floor in our shack. She would come back to the graveyard whenever she was hungry, and father would take her in. When he asked her where she came from, he found out that she was the daughter of one of his former servants, a man who had denounced him during the People's Court. In fact, she cringed

when he told her who he was, a former wealthy landowner with ten
servants in his household. But he told her not to be afraid. 'We're
equal now,' he said. 'Think of the one million people already dead
from starvation. You and I are blessed.' He would drink himself into
a stupor every night, and then one night he took the girl outside our
shack and they slept there. From then on he never slept inside when
the girl came. Then one morning I woke to her cries. I ran out and
saw her weeping over his body. I found snakebite marks on his leg.
Even the girl did not know what happened to him, and so I believed
that he died in his stupor."

Chi Lan rubs her arm. "That's very sad, *chú*," she says.

"I was worried when I saw you lying out there."

"What if someone here is bitten by a poisonous snake?"

"The old woman has antidote. There's a jar in the refrigerator. It
has a label in both Vietnamese and English."

She laughs. "*Chú*, I promise I won't mistake it for the cooking
broth."

A bead of water rolls down the side of her face. She hunches up
one shoulder and dries her cheek with her shirt. My shirt. Breathing
in sharply she says, "Now I smell of tobacco. Just like you."

A Mother's Tale

Yesterday I took Mrs. Rossi to Ông Doc town to see a doctor. She was running a fever. Both mother and daughter were in the doctor's office, and I was there with them as an interpreter. It could be the sun, or insect bite, the doctor said. The forest can be a scourge.

I translated what the old doctor said. He administered an intravenous antibiotic and Mrs. Rossi rested for a while. When we came out on the street, the forenoon sun was so strong she stood back on the curbside and donned her straw hat. She looked darker now, but not because her face was shaded. She'd gotten peasants' skin from riding day after day in the sampan and going into the forest. Her crow's feet showed in deep grooves when she squinted to watch a wedding procession going down the street. Standing hunched, hand locked in Chi Lan's, Mrs. Rossi still had that quiet, determined look. I wondered how much longer before those soft blue eyes would lose their dogged expression.

Water was receding on the street after a hard rain, and a wind-born stink came from the waterfront where fish were being sun-dried. Chi Lan pointed toward the procession. "Mom, look!" The bride in her long white dress stood before a large puddle of water. The procession stopped. Then the bridegroom and the best man hoisted her up and carried her across the street, not even rolling up their pants legs. The rest followed, sloshing through the water. You could hear everyone laughing.

Mrs. Rossi smiled. She looked tired but relaxed. Perhaps being here with her daughter, instead of the forest, brought her enjoyment. We walked back to where I parked the Peugeot, and the noise the swiftlets made in the bird colonies made her cock her head. Chi Lan explained to her about the chirpings as she held her mother's hand, both finding their steps on the rough parts of the incline of the street, where broken pavement was patched with hewed logs of mangrove and date palm. We stopped at the café, also a brothel, and I bought them each a *café sua da*, the Vietnamese iced coffee with a dash of condensed milk. I knew Chi Lan had told her about the upstairs rooms with red-bulb wreathed window shutters in pink, because Mrs. Rossi kept looking back.

The port was empty of the fishing boats. "Where have they gone?" Mrs. Rossi asked. I told her that after the full moon, all the boats would head out to sea for days. "Why after the full moon?" she asked. Before that time, I told her, the water was moonlit and fish wouldn't bite the bait, so all the fishermen stayed in town getting drunk day and night, and the brothel was as busy as a soup kitchen. Then when the moon became a waning crescent, the boats were unmoored, and one by one they left the river port, taking with them the owl's eyes painted on both sides of the bow, those wakeful eyes day and night having longed for the return to the sea.

*

Back at the inn, I hung a hammock on the veranda for Mrs. Rossi to take her siesta. I gave her a glass of iced lemonade. She stayed the swing with her bare feet and took a healthy swig. With one leg stretched out, she pulled up her pants leg. "Giang, look," she said. "Your tobacco water is a wonderful remedy. I wore socks I soaked in that water and no leeches have bothered me since."

I was glad to see no fresh bite marks on her ankles. I asked her if she felt any better from the fever and she nodded, pressing the chilled glass against the side of her face, flushed from the afternoon heat.

Chi Lan came out with two glasses of lemonade. She handed me one and sat down on the floor, knees drawn to her chest. The heat glimmered above the road and the air quivered. You could hear the cicadas singing in the tree tops, pulsing across the air, in the tangles of hummingbird trees, sea almond trees, and palm trees. The ethereal cadence at times died down, then suddenly flared up. I asked if they had ever seen bamboo flowering, and Chi Lan, gazing at the grove, asked, "Is it true that soon after they flower they will die?"

"Yes," I said. "Some species flower every one hundred years, and those of the same kind flower simultaneously all over the world. I saw the bamboo flower one day in the forest when I was your age."

"The massive flowering?" she asked.

"Yes," I said, "the once-in-a-lifetime phenomenon." I told them about the moment the greenish-yellow pods opened, and the petals unfurled, mauve and trembling, and every clump of golden bamboo turned pale purple.

Mrs. Rossi shook her head, smiling. "I won't live long enough to see such a wonder."

*

In the evening we sat on the veranda, the air now cool, and the breeze brought a scent of mud from a canal across the land. Mrs. Rossi reclined in the hammock, her loose shirt untucked, hanging down to her thighs, its whiteness a pale luster in the dark. Chi Lan and I sat in the metal folding chairs, looking toward the road. Mrs. Rossi said she was thinking of Maggie and her husband. She really liked Maggie, whom she called "a barrel of fun." The Irish couple had left that morning. Before leaving, Maggie held Mrs. Rossi's face in her hands and said, "This is awful. Ya should quit going into de forest and see de trees. Dat's right, love. At your age ya should rest. Ya should drink plenty tamahtoe juice and take plenty vihtamin. I wish ya find what ya lookin for over dere."

I told Mrs. Rossi I would miss the sound of Maggie's laugh. Chi Lan reminded me that I forgot to cook a dish of snake meat for them. She looked toward the road. A street peddler was pushing his cart and a boy, silhouetted against the glowing lantern hung behind him on the cart, was walking and striking his bamboo clappers. The *tok-tok-tok* kept cadence with his steps. I said, "You must try that man's noodle soup."

"Pho?" Chi Lan said.

"No, *hu tieu*. Chinese-style noodle soup."

"I'd love to try it," Chi Lan said. "Mom?"

"Sure, dear," Mrs. Rossi said. "Anything."

The man pushed the cart to the veranda. I asked for three bowls. The boy sat down on his haunches, gazing up at Chi Lan, who clicked her camera while the man prepared the dishes. He sliced the pork belly into thin cuts, pinched a handful of egg noodles, and dropped them into the boiling iron pot, then quickly strained them and placed them into a bowl. His hands deftly garnished the bowl with the meat, bean sprouts, sautéed garlic, and shallots. He wiped his hands on the rag hung on the handlebar and arranged three wontons on top of the bowl and squeezed a lemon wedge on it. Ceremoniously, he ladled the pork-based broth, his head tilted watching the ladle hover and empty itself. Steam rose from the bowl in the wavering lantern light. A pungent fragrance wafted up to the veranda. The man fitted the bowl with a pair of chopsticks and a spoon, and the boy carried the dish up. I told him to give the first bowl to Mrs. Rossi.

"Do you want to sit at his cart and eat?" I asked her.

"Sure," she said. "I want to try that."

She walked barefoot down the steps to the cart and the man pulled out a folding wooden chair for her. She placed the bowl on the metal ledge and motioned for us to join her. We sat at the cart, watching the man prepare each bowl, the air warm and wet with the noodle odor.

After we were done eating and the noodle cart left, the *tok-tok-tok* of the bamboo clappers fading into the distance, I made *café sua da* for each of us and we sat in the dark, sipping coffee. Above the creaking of her hammock, Mrs. Rossi said, "It's so beautiful here. Sometimes it makes me wonder why life is so complicated."

"You mean this rural life?" I asked.

"Yes." She put her glass on the veranda floor. "My son told me about this river. Around here somewhere. Said it was covered with white water lilies and full of fragrance. I wish I could see it the way he saw it. Just once. So help me God."

"Can we take her there when she's well again?" Chi Lan asked me.

"Certainly," I said. To Mrs. Rossi, I added, "You cross that river just about every day when Ông Ba takes you to the forest in his sampan."

Mrs. Rossi sat up, lifted her glass. "That river we came in from the canal? That's the same river my son told me about?"

"Ma'am," I said, "that's the Trem River. You'll see the stretch with water lilies farther up toward Upper U Minh. They used to grow so wild they covered the river with only a narrow passage for boats, and when the flowers are in full bloom you could smell their scents way upriver and downriver."

"It must look like a painting," Mrs. Rossi said, "the way he described."

"I'm sure he must have had an artistic eye."

Mrs. Rossi sipped her iced coffee and, palming her glass in her lap, gazed into the night. "Look at that!"

In the bamboo grove a blue light glowed, drifting knee high above the ground. The night was so dark the incandescent blue looked eerie, hovering in that stillness.

"What is that?" Chi Lan asked.

"The blue-ghost fireflies," I said. "It's their mating season."

"Fireflies?" Mrs. Rossi asked. "Why aren't they blinking?"

"They are not the ordinary fireflies," I said. "Not the flashing ones. They only glow. The males."

"Those lights are from the males?"

"Well, the females glow too. But they don't have wings. They stay on the ground. They need much moisture and ground cover. During the day both males and females hide under the leaves on the ground. I used to see them when I was deep in the forest."

"So if you destroy the ground and the forest," Mrs. Rossi said, "like the war did, then you destroy them too. Am I right?"

"Especially the females," I said. "They can't fly."

"Especially the females," Mrs. Rossi said. "The source of life."

"They're beautiful," Chi Lan said.

She picked up her camera she'd left under her chair. She knelt on one knee on the top step, clicking off several shots, and the flashlights made quick bright bursts. "They're like winged ghosts," Chi Lan said.

I coughed into my hand as Chi Lan turned to look at me. I had refrained from smoking whenever I was with her. Mrs. Rossi returned to her hammock, swinging it side to side.

"Yesterday," she said, "Mr. Lung and I encountered something very bizarre in the forest. We saw under a tree a heap of dirt shaped like a sitting human. Mr. Lung explained that it was a termite mound. I said, 'What's inside?' He tapped it with his spade and the dirt mound started to fall apart, and Holy Jesus, it's a human skeleton. A sitting skeleton carrying a rucksack. The rucksack, too, was encased completely in dirt." She held up her hand. "Giang, I know what you're about to ask. It was a North Vietnamese soldier, from what Mr. Lung saw in the rucksack. But there was nothing to indicate his name or where he had lived."

Mrs. Rossi said she felt devastated when she thought of the dead soldier's family, who might still be searching for him, or waiting for him to come home. She wondered where all the souls of the dead have gone. I told her perhaps the ghosts needed a medium to show themselves to the living, and the fireflies' blue lights were that medium, just like earth, water, fire, and air made up the medium of living human beings. Mrs. Rossi said she had never believed in ghosts, but after going into the U Minh forest she wasn't so certain anymore. She said once in the forest, in a damp, shaded place she had sensed somebody's presence. She got goose bumps. She said she believed the woman inn owner's story about the sound of human crying in the forest on rainy nights following a muggy day that made the air thick like vapors rising from the bogs, and the vaporous air was the right medium for otherworldly manifestation. I told them the story of five hundred French paratroopers who were dropped into the U Minh forest in 1952. All of them disappeared in the mangrove swamps forever. "One night recently," I said, "I was standing at the window of my room smoking a cigarette and the night was full of the sawing of crickets, the clicking of bats, the harsh squawking of night herons up in their tree colony. As I listened mindlessly to them, I heard a thump, then another. There I saw two clods of dirt resting on the window ledge. How they landed precisely side by side I did not know. Neither did I know where they came from. The following night it happened again. I had to tell the woman inn owner about the incidents. She said, 'They want to be fed.' 'Who?' I asked. 'The dead people,' she said. So she put on the rear veranda a bowl of cooked rice, a plate of boiled chicken, a bundle of bananas, lidded with a dome cover. After that there were no more clods of dirt."

Mrs. Rossi said she believed that through the praying and worshipping we keep in touch with the spirits of those who are gone. She said she saw many shrines in the land and understood that they remind us of things beyond us. But she said God will hear you only if you are sincere in your praying, because faith is something not seen, not touched, therefore not explicable to mortals.

It was the first time I saw her cry.

*

There wasn't a soul on the moonlit road that went by the inn as I returnd from Mr. Rum's place. A fisherman, he was Old Lung's drinking buddy. I carried a burlap bag in the crook of my arm. Nearing midnight, the moon hovered directly overhead, a beautiful round disk in a cloudless sky, and the road glowed softly in yellow. In that pale light you could see along the road the cajeput flowers white as milk and you could smell their scent light as the lotus'.

The road bent and, ahead of me after the curve, a peddler's cart was moving along, the *tok-tok-tok* of a bamboo block sounding like the Buddhist wooden percussion. A cart selling fresh corn. I walked faster until I came within earshot to hear the portable radio music coming from the cart. At this hour, mother and daughter must be sound asleep. They had never tried the local sweet corn. The woman peddler pushed the cart along with one hand on the handlebar, the other hand tapping the bamboo block with a wooden stick. She passed by here now and then, always late at night, and always there were customers who got hungry around this time. The cart-fitted blue umbrella, on this clear night, was furled around a tall metal pole behind the handlebar.

Past the inn, a voice called out from the veranda. Chi Lan's voice. It startled me. I clutched the bag tighter. I told the woman peddler that I worked at the inn and my late-night guests would like to try her sweet corn. I walked beside the cart through the entrance crowned with bamboo and I could see both mother and daughter standing on the veranda.

"*Chú*," Chi Lan called to me. Her voice was soft with a lilt in "*chú*." Uncle.

"Giang!" Mrs. Rossi raised her voice. "Are you a street peddler now?"

They both laughed. I smiled at them. I felt sad but happy at the same time. Happy to see Mrs. Rossi in good spirits. Happy to see her smile. In a white nightgown she stood barefoot, reclasping the hairband behind her ears, her hair and gown startlingly white. Chi Lan walked down the steps. Also barefoot, she wore white shorts and a red T-shirt. She didn't look sleepy.

"Where've you been, *chú*?" she asked and dropped her gaze at the burlap bag in my arm.

"I was visiting friends."

"Is that a sleeping bag?"

"No." I put my other arm on it. "Just some stuff."

"We got hungry and Mom didn't want to ask the old woman for snacks. They're in bed now."

"I know." I tried to smile. "I thought you would both be in bed too."

"Well." Giggling, she looked up to her room and back at me. "You know why I'm still up?"

"Why?"

"There's a bat in our room."

Mrs. Rossi coughed to interrupt her. She said, "Dear, you're holding up the lady."

Chi Lan put her hand to her mouth. "I'm sorry."

I moved to the side of the cart by the gas lamp. "What can they have, sis?" I asked.

"That depends," the woman laid down the stick in her hand. "Do they like boiled corn? Or roasted? With butter and fried onions? Or stir-fried corn?"

I told Chi Lan the choices.

"What's stir-fried corn?" she asked.

"They break loose the kernels and stir-fry them."

"I'll have one roasted corn."

"I'll try stir-fry," Mrs. Rossi called down. "I've never tried that."

"What do you have, *chú*?" Chi Lan asked me.

"I already ate," I said, avoiding her gaze. But I felt hungry again, or perhaps it was the gnawing in my stomach. My throat felt so dry it hurt when I swallowed. She stood with me watching the woman lay a corn ear on the coal brazier, fanning it with a hand fan until the coals came to life, burning bright red. While the corn was being roasted, she placed a skillet on a portable gas grill, turned up the flame and quickly poured some cooking oil onto the skillet. She turned the corn ear on the brazier, one side palely browned, and fanned the coals, and the warm air smelled of burned matchsticks from coal smoke. She emptied a plastic container onto the skillet as the oil began bubbling. The kernels, yellow and wedge-shaped, popped merrily. Chi Lan swept her hair back behind her ears and watched the woman cut a thin slice of fresh butter from a stick she stored in an ice box, and the butter melted instantly into a sizzling yellow puddle, the butter-rich air tinged with coal smoke. The woman sprinkled some diced onions and added a pinch of sugar, salt, and powder red pepper. She stirred the kernels quickly, so the heat only shrank the onions into curly clumps of light brown, the kernels glistening with butter and red-pepper flecks. She lowered the flame, let the skillet sit, and turned the corn on the brazier until the ear browned evenly. She pulled and cut a large sheet of aluminum foil and, with a brush, smeared the foil with melted butter from a can and stopped when the sheet glazed over with yellow streaks. As we watched, she coated the butter-filmed foil evenly with salt and pepper, picked up the corn by the shank and wrapped it tightly in the foil.

We sat on the veranda in the dark after the peddler was gone, each of us having a glass of fresh lemonade that Chi Lan made earlier in the evening. The moon washed the land with a dreamy yellow, soft as a veil. The buttered smell of corn lingered in the air and I felt the gnawing in my stomach again. Mrs. Rossi, sitting on a chair by the hammock and eating with a spoon out of the carry-out container, said the stir-fried corn was delicious. She asked me what I had for dinner. I told her I had blood cockles at Mr. Rum's. Chi Lan chimed in, "I'd love to try blood cockles, but not the liquor." Mrs. Rossi chuckled. "Dear, they go together. At least that's how I remember." Chi Lan explained to me that her mother used to drink. That her drinking became heavier after her son went missing in the war. I asked Mrs. Rossi about her husband. After a silence she said that he killed himself. Her tone gave me pause. I touched the burlap bag under my chair with my foot and dragged it in closer to me. "Why," I asked. Mrs. Rossi closed the carton, wiped her lips with the back of her hand. "After the war," she said. "He never really came back."

I sighed. I wanted to get up and walked out into the night, filling my lungs with fresh air, and I wanted to walk down the moonlit road like a man who occasionally takes to the road with nothing on his mind.

Chi Lan wrapped up the finished corn in the foil. Its faint rustle broke the quiet. "You should've tried the roast corn, *chú*."

"You enjoyed it?"

"So tasty. I'm fascinated with the street peddlers around here."

"I knew you and your mom would love the fresh corn they sell from the cart."

"I love corn. Do you, *chú*?"

"Yeah. How many kernels on a single ear?"

Chi Lan turned her head toward me. Mrs. Rossi said, "Good question, Giang. I know the answer but let her try first."

"That's a weird question," Chi Lan said, giggling. "Who could've thought of that?"

"Well," I said, "how many?"

"I don't know, *chú*." She grabbed my hand. "You call the woman peddler back. I'll order another corn ear and I'll tell you how many."

"Want me to tell you?"

"Please. I learn new things every day here."

"Eight hundred on a single ear."

Mrs. Rossi weighed in. "A thousand on a healthy ear of corn. How many rows do you think each ear might have, Giang?"

Chi Lan turned to her mother. "Mom!"

"I used to teach, remember, dear?" Mrs. Rossi said, smiling.

"Sixteen, ma'am," I said. "Roughly."

"You're right," Mrs. Rossi said.

"You're good, *chú*," Chi Lan said, placing the foil-wrapped corn at her feet.

"What did you do today?" I asked her.

"I went out with my camera. You know what I photographed in the back of the inn?"

"Did you wear a long-sleeved shirt?"

"Yes, *chú*. I remember the wasp sting." She averted her gaze when she saw me looking steadily at her. "I photographed the red-vine spinach."

"They're the old woman's prize. I put up the poles so they can climb on them."

"They're so beautiful in the sun. Those red-stemmed, red-veined leaves in close-up shots. They're green on the sun-facing side, but I didn't know they were pale purple on the underside."

"They have berries now. Did you see them?"

"Oh yes. I took a few pictures of those."

I told her I loved the dark-red stains from those berries when she crushed them in her hand, an intense purple color, darker than beet juice. I said I would love to see her photographs someday. Maybe her photographs would help keep alive my memory of her. I wanted to preserve those memories, pure as honey, as long as I lived.

She seemed to want to say something but held back.

"Did you close the window shutters before you went to bed?" I asked her.

"No, *chú*. I left them open for fresh air."

"And you saw the bat fly in?"

"No, *chú*. I saw a black thing on the wall." She laughed lightly. "Now I know why they painted all the walls white. So you can spot centipedes or ants. Or bats. That bat is the size of a lemon. First I thought it was a giant moth. Then up close I saw it wasn't a moth. And that ugly thing was hanging on top of the door frame."

"I'll get it."

"I told my mom, *Chú* can get this ugly thing out of our room, and she said she hasn't seen you all evening."

"It was my day off."

"I couldn't fall asleep. Good grief. Have you ever listened to those house lizards at night? They make those *tak-tak-tak* sounds. Always three. Then again. *Tak-tak-tak*."

I chuckled. I loved listening to her melodious voice. Clear, lilting.

"You know something else, *chú*," she said. "You won't notice how the hour hand on a clock moves, even if you lie there with your eyes open and try to see if the hour hand moves. I swear to God, it never moved and after a while I got up."

"Were you afraid the bat might drop down on you?"

"No. But the notion of having that hairy creature in my room scares me."

"I had one in my room, a big one, the first night I came here. Back then, window shutters were never closed. The old woman just forgot. She didn't tell me where I was supposed to sleep either. So I asked her, Where do I sleep tonight? And she said, Where? Here I've got four hectares of land and you can pick any place out there to sleep if you can't find a place in the house."

Both Chi Lan and Mrs. Rossi laughed. "She's a little sour most of the time," Chi Lan said.

"She's a good old woman," I said. "If you get to know her. By the way, ma'am, when you feel like visiting places again, I'll take you and Chi Lan to the Trem River near Upper U Minh."

"Where we can see the white water lilies?" Mrs. Rossi said.

"Yes, ma'am."

"That'd be lovely," Mrs. Rossi said. "Before we go back home."

"Go back home?" I said with a start.

"Very soon. I'm still tired. So I'll rest for a few more days."

Chi Lan turned to look at me. "My mom doesn't want to go back into the forest anymore. I wanted to tell you that today."

Mrs. Rossi rose and went to the hammock. Sitting down slowly to find her balance, she said, "But I'd love to go see that river of white water lilies. I really would. Just once."

Her voice was strained. She put her hand on her forehead, half reclining in the hammock.

I rose from the chair and knelt on one knee by the hammock. "Ma'am," I said.

"Yes, Giang." She peered down at me, her voice scratchy.

I looked down at my feet, at the floor, then I looked back up at her. "I have something to tell you. I found the remains of your son."

"What?" Her hand dropped from her face. "What did you say?"

I felt the presence of Chi Lan over me. "The old man I visited today . . . he buried your son . . . after he found him in a creek the night he died."

"What?" Mrs. Rossi tried to sit up. "Lord Jesus. What are you telling me, Giang?"

"Your son has been laid to rest . . . on that man's land for twenty years now. I was telling him about your ordeal . . . Then he told me over the years he'd buried a few people here on his land. Dead. Unclaimed. Drowned in the ocean and drifted ashore." I rose, picked up the burlap bag and brought it to the hammock. "In here, ma'am. All his personal effects. Wallet, dog tag, wristwatch, the rain poncho he wore on the night he died."

Mrs. Rossi leaned back, as if afraid to touch the bag. Suddenly she shook her head repeatedly. "What's going on?" Her voice cracked.

Chi Lan bent over her mother, gathered her hands into her own. "Mom!" her voice sounded thick.

Mrs. Rossi brushed her hand across her eyes. She stared at the faded green bag. Heaving, she said, "Can I see what's in it? Can I?"

"Let me get the lamp," I said.

When I came back out, holding the gas lamp chest high, Mrs. Rossi was clutching the burlap bag, pressing her cheek against its rough texture, and Chi Lan was kneeling at her feet.

I set the lamp on the floor. "Ma'am, you want me to take them out for you?"

Mrs. Rossi said nothing. She reluctantly gave the bag over. I pulled the poncho out, crinkled and smelly, and she pulled it to her chest, sniffing the dark fabric, stroking it. I held the dog tag and the opened wallet with her son's picture for her to see in the light. Her lips crimped. She looked at them, then suddenly tears filled her eyes and she sobbed. "God. Oh God. Oh Lord God." Her voice choked, she sobbed, and Chi Lan cradled her mother's head in her arms and cried over her mother.

I sat looking at my feet, at the lamp casting a yellow oblong on the floor. When Mrs. Rossi finally gathered herself, she reached out and seized my hand and squeezing it she said, "Bless you, Giang. Bless your heart. Can you take me to his grave tomorrow?"

I nodded. "Of course."

"I want to thank the man who had laid my son to rest," Mrs. Rossi said.

"Yes, ma'am," I say softly.

Mrs. Rossi wiped her eyes and her nose with the heel of her hand. "I guess nobody knows what happened to my son. How he ended that way in a creek. Dear God, do I want to know?"

I raised my face to her, my whole being tensed. "Ma'am. I know how he died."

I put her son's wallet in her hands, then the dog tag, then the wristwatch. I explained to her that Mr. Rum, the fisherman, found her son's corpse drifting in from somewhere and caught in his fish trap. Her son was wearing a rain poncho. The date Mr. Rum told me woke up in me the memory of that fateful night. Time suddenly shrank. Twenty years was merely a blink of an eye. I told Mrs. Rossi that her son's base camp was responsible for many of our North Vietnamese combat losses and casualties, because it controlled the whole stretch of Trem River that cuts through the U Minh forest.

That night when our battalions attacked his base we were to leave
no survivors. I told her that it was me and my men who got into the
forest chasing him in the torrential rain until we spotted him near
a creek. He was unarmed. We shot him. Just as he turned around
facing us. Got him in the throat. We kicked his body into the water
and left. "I was me, ma'am," I said to her. "I shot him. I didn't know
until tonight who he was."

"No, Giang. No. This can't be true."

"It was a terrible day, twenty years ago. It pains me now beyond
words."

Her hands shaking, Mrs. Rossi wept, pressing her son's
belongings to her chest. I bowed my head. I cried. I cried for his
youth and mine, lost, wasted. I cried for mothers like Mrs. Rossi
whose lives ebbed and flowed with the hope that their sons would
someday be found, what's left of them, so they can hold them again
like they did on the day they were born. Tears rolled down my face.
Crying for lives so broken. I felt Mrs. Rossi's hands touching my
head, pulling me to her and, gently, I rested my head in her lap as if
she were the mother I never had. And we held each other. In that
eternity.

The Leper Colony

The letter said, "Madame Thi Lan is very ill. Be kindly advised of our necessary action to be taken for gravely ill residents. This will be the only correspondence from this office to our resident's family concerned. Respectfully." Having taken ten days by postal mail, it arrived from the village office that oversaw the leper colony where her mother had been an inhabitant for the past three years.

*

The last time, seven years now, they were together was in an afternoon when her mother took her to a seaside town to meet her husband-to-be. She was seventeen. It was on a ferry in Central Vietnam of her hometown that the man had seen her. Crossing the river that day to her school. Later in the day his chauffeur in a white shirt and black pants had politely asked her at the school recess that someone would like to have a few words with her. That someone was a man triple her age. An overlord from the deep south of the Mekong Delta. He stayed at a hotel. That night he sent his chauffeur to pick up both her and her mother. Her mother, a schoolteacher then, in a traditional *áo dài* the color of yellow cocoon silk, looked timid as she greeted him. The man wore a charcoal gray three-piece suit; a white silk handkerchief peeked from his breast pocket. In a white blouse and navy-blue skirt, she looked like a French schoolgirl, the man complimented her.

At the pier of the seaside town that afternoon, they could see the chauffeur already waiting beside the black Mercedes at the top of the steps.

"Let me take her around the town," her mother said to the chauffeur. "You can come, if you wish."

"I'll be right here, ma'am," the chauffeur said. "I think I should."

Barges cluttered the waterway and fishing nets threw silhouettes across the fiery water. She breathed in the metallic tang of fish, the wetly sweet smell of rot timbers, of boats and barges and waterlogged wooden stilts. Overhead crows circled, cawing noisily. Some came down flapping their wings in front of the slaughterhouse that sat back from the street. The birds waddled, preening themselves, waiting for throwaways of guts that butchers tossed out.

A liveliness seeped through her veins. This would be her new home.

The Main Street clanged with noises and sounds. Little shops of Chinese and Indians sat among local stores. See the porters bent under those bales of garments? Yellow and gaunt and barefooted. See them pull the two-wheeled carts on their cranelike legs? Half naked, oxblood skin covered with sweat. See the grimy children stand bare to their waists laughing? Gaps in their teeth, snots in their eyes. She would belong here, this race, this people.

The street was narrow and jammed with huge baskets sitting on wooden trestles. Women vendors gawked at her, talking among themselves after she went past. An American middle-aged man nodded slightly at her. *Hello there*, he said. Nodding, she greeted him.

They passed stalls selling delicacies and confections and she felt her stomach gnaw. Maybe she should eat something, for all she had since breakfast was a bowl of rice gruel.

Now the sights of confections tempted her and she stopped in front of a stall set against the loam-packed wall of a hut. A little girl came out of nowhere carrying a child astride her hip. The child's nose was smeared with snot, her dark velvety eyes rheumy. They gazed at her and at her mother whose face was shadowed by a palm-leaf conical hat. Then their gaze dropped at the assortments of preserved fruits on wooden trays. Tangerines, plum, dates, tamarinds.

She said to the girl, "What do you like," and the girl looked up at her, surprised, and put her finger between her lips, sizing up the sweets. Then she pointed at a tray lined with round barley sugar, each sandwiched by round rice papers the size of a fig.

"I see," she said and then to the confectioner, "five, please."

While she paid, she watched the girl take the barley sugar wrapped in paper and held the bag as if she didn't know it was given to her. "Eat," she said, pinching an imaginary confection and putting it into her mouth. The confectioner grinned as they watched the girl open the paper, pick one candy and let the child lick it.

Sunlight had become mild and shadows grown on the street and across the water. When they went back up the street, a crowd of people was gathering on the sidewalk. People turned their heads to gaze at the two of them and then stepped back to give them a view.

She looked down at an American man lying on his back, his face beet-red, drooling like a baby.

"He aint dead," a woman said and someone repeated, "No, he aint dead, just drunk out of his skull."

Her mother searched for the bottle. "Drunk?"

A woman spat red saliva of betel chew and wiped her swollen lips with the back of her hand. "Drank *chum-chum* over there. I saw him. Came out here talking to himself . . . looked like a madman."

Her gaze lingered on the man lying still at her feet. An olive visor cap sat cock-eyed on top of his head.

"He'll die," her mother said. "Call the authorities."

"Sis," the woman said, "he'll be all right. These fools ruin their health because they've heard of this *chum-chum*'s notoriety. It could pass for poison this rice liquor the locals brew. All sorts of impurities are let through during distillation. But cheap. And lethal."

She took one last look at the man, his mouth still foaming. When they left, walking back toward the pier, she turned to her mother. "I guess these men don't have families here."

"Yes, darling. It adds up when you're alone."

She began to know that feeling—alone in a strange place away from home.

*

By midmorning two days later, after the letter's arrival, her boat reached a bend in the river winding like an S and after another bend they entered an open space filled with sandbanks. A wall of gigantic bamboos swallowed them with their tall, thick trunks throwing their shade out on water. In their blue shade was a lonesome promontory.

A large red flag fluttered in the breeze at the tip of the landing. She leaned out from under the cane-laced dome and said to the guide, "There the red flag. I recognize it now."

"What's it for, Ma'am?" the guide said.

"It cautions travelers. There's a leper hamlet up beyond. Listen, we're in the vicinity of my destination."

He rose from the bench and found his balance toward the cabin where she sat. An enormous man in his fifties, hired by her husband to escort her to the leper hamlet, he now lowered himself to sit on the narrow bench, his hands resting on his knees, and, without looking at her, spoke, "Ma'am, are you really ready for this?"

"I am." Her eyes squinted at the empty promontory and, as the boat passed it, she said, "How do we get there? I forgot. It's been two years."

The guide asked the brown-garbed boatman standing at the stern and ordered him to find an entry to the hamlet, for the promontory was barricaded with a wooden stockade. They went under the shade of bamboos feathering the sandbanks and found a stream hemmed in by inclines yellowed with reeds and castor beans. Out of the bamboo shade the boat followed the stream and sunlight gilded the mist with glitters like gold dust on the banks. Both the boatman and his wife rowed silently in the harsh cries of peacocks calling one another behind the hillocks, and, up on a hill where breadfruit trees stood laden with their pendulous fruits, they saw the ruin of a pagoda charred by fire.

There was no entry but a steep climb etched into the clay soil by stones and rotten logs. The boatman and his wife rested their oars while the guide helped her find her footing up the perilous steps. In fact, she helped him find his balance on the treacherously narrow rungs by making him look up, not down, as they ascended the stairs. Somewhere on the face on the sheer slope, where maidenhair fern leaned out for sun from every cleft, they saw above them a family of black gibbons seating themselves on a bed of rocks, tranquil like fixtures of rock themselves. When the guide rose enormously from below, they shot into the woods like hallucinations.

A trail led them into the woods past the abandoned pagoda and brought them in front of a bamboo stockade. There was a hut outside the latched gate. She waited under the shade of a mangrove as the guide approached the hut. The landscape began appearing familiar to her. She saw a human figure stir up in the dim hovel. Moments later the guide came back and told her the hut was used as the infirmary to treat the lepers for their sores, malaria and dysentery. Neighboring villages shared the medical costs. Here it also received food relatives from those villages brought for the lepers, and the food would be taken into the hamlet and placed outside the lepers' huts.

A man came out of the hut. A small, middle-aged man with an awed look on his face as he stood in front of the guests. He kept scratching his head, his small eyes darting back and forth between them, and he stammered when he spoke. She gave him her mother's name, and he said he did not know. She asked him of a woman named Thi Lan and he shook his head at the name. He said someone from the village might know, because he was just a hired hand from another village.

"Nobody wants this kind of job," he said. "I don't mind."

"What did you do before?" the guide asked.

"I . . . I went from one place to another, sir. I begged."

"And now you treat the lepers for their ailments?" she said.

"That's right, ma'am. They have all kinds. But sores are what bother them most."

"What kind of lesions?" she asked.

"Holes on their legs, ma'am. Sometimes on their bodies." He pointed to his abdomen. "I bind them up and . . . and they'd come back the next day. Same spots. Asked them what happened to the gauze I tied those sores with. Don't know, they always say. I know what they did with those bandages. They took them off and used them as handkerchief. Yeah. The long one they wrapped round their head. Keep head cold away, they said."

Her eyes turned pensive. "I saw the warning flag on the promontory. What's the reason to barricade it? It wasn't there two years ago. How can they wash themselves? Where do they get water?"

The man shook his head. "Ma'am, it's blocked all around so they can't get out and go into the villages to beg. It's a long story. They used to come down there to get water for cooking. Yeah. To bathe. But some drowned in the river 'cause they couldn't swim. And then some slept there 'cause it's a long way to hobble back. Ma'am, many of them have no legs. The tigers ate them. And once those tigers knew where to get their meals, they'd keep coming back."

She sighed as she looked into the hamlet through chinks in the stockade. "They told me last time they moved my mother to another place. How can we find out where she is in the hamlet?"

The man simply looked at her and then at the guide.

"Ma'am," the guide said, "I wonder if you can even recognize her if you find her again."

The man rubbed his nose a few times and said, "You can go into the hamlet. Just don't let them follow you out."

"Why?" The guide knitted his brows.

"They do that, sir. Sometimes they got out cause some visitors took pity on them and find a place for them in some leprosarium."

She nodded. "We understand. But if anyone of us were like them, wouldn't we wish for a chance to be cared for?"

The man said nothing and dropped his gaze. She gestured toward the shut gate. "Would you let us in?"

The man threw open the latch and the gate creaked swinging on a half arc. As she entered the hamlet with the guide, the man said, "There're two men from this village in there. They just came in. You can ask them."

Green and yellow were the only colors in the bamboo forest. Ocher was the color of footpaths feathered with thin leaves the pale green of grasshoppers. In the quiet they heard the peacocks again, answering one another from some unseen bushes, and the melancholy creaking of bamboo trunks. She told the guide to keep walking and not to bother with her trailing behind. She told him bamboos were masters of their habitats where no other plants could grow, so a walk in a bamboo forest was easy. Yet he walked half-turned, eyeing the ground, wary of broken bamboo thorns.

Then the first hut came into sight, then another, nested under tall giant trunks of bamboo, shadowed by their laced tops so that they sat like toy huts sheltered by a canopy of smoky green. On each crude palm-woven door, most of them shut, was hung a square, white cloth numbered in black ink. Looking at them she thought perhaps that was how food was brought to each hut. By the door of each hut sat a wicker basket, its handle dangling with a small white cloth inked with a number. She understood that the inhabitants were fed—how often she did not know—unlike in some leper hamlets where the lepers were left on their own to raise fowls and pigs and scavenge for foods in the forest.

When the trail had led them far into the hamlet, at times winding around thick bamboo trunks the size of a man's leg, at times skirting bamboo hedges hollowed at the base with openings so that peering through them they saw the dwellers, they stopped at what they saw.

Lepers had come out in front of their huts, as if they had watched the trail for visitors. They materialized from behind the giant bamboo trunks, emerging through man-sized holes in the hedges. Limbless dwarfs, hideous deformed humans. Some limped, some crawled, some were pushed sitting on little box carts, some, blind, were led by the hand.

Her voice restrained, she told the guide to keep walking, while her gaze fell upon looming faces filled with livid sores, lumpy with red knots, hollowed with purplish cavities. She heard the guide. He told the inhabitants to keep off the trail and yet they came closer. Looking down she saw eyes like fishes', many filmed with mucus, faces like masks because their skins had gone dead, hands with nubbed fingers because their tips had been eaten away by leprosy. Those hands were bent like claws. She felt them tugging at the hems of her dress. She kept walking, hands clutching the sides of her dress. Pity made her want to stop, perhaps because she was pulling away.

The guide's voice startled her. He ordered the lepers to back off. They relented. Now the cortege trailed them the best they knew how. Grotesque cripples on stumpy legs, crook-backed mutants in swinging gait.

She followed the enormous guide, seeing his broad back, shielded by his huge body. The strange noises of the lepers' bodies made in their motion, of their laborious breathing. The sights of their hovels, those animal's lairs, so low only the lepers could enter because most of them trundled themselves on hands. She thought of those who had been here, like herself and the guide, those who showed mercy and took lepers to a more human haven.

She heard gibberish of sounds. A commotion. Then a crackling noise. Ahead, off the trail, thin columns of smoke spiraled up the great tall trunks of bamboo and soon the air smelled foul. A hut was burning. Closer she stood, hands clenched, watching two men throwing bundles of straw and twigs around the hut. Flames licked the thatch roof and rose in blue and orange and the roof popped noisily and began to sway. Suddenly a figure stirred inside the inferno. Like an effigy set on fire. Watching, she thought her soul was being sucked away by horror. A leper still alive inside the hut. It staggered to the blazing door and fell. The fire roared, ashes swirled, black smoke pumped in furious blasts up the sky. She could smell the stench of burned woods and straw and flesh.

When the fire died down and the ground was a black pile of debris and charred woods, the two men, spade in hand, approached the body. They turned to look at the visitors who came toward them. Behind them the lepers watched.

"Are you gentlemen from the village?" the guide asked.

"Yessir," one man said, leaning on his spade.

"We're looking for someone here. Perhaps you know her."

"Yessir."

"A former schoolteacher."

The men looked at each other.

"Her common name is Thi Lan," she said, seeing their confused look.

The man who leaned on his spade scratched his ear and then,

hesitatingly, pointed at the charred corpse. "There she is, ma'am."

She felt a shortness of breath. She blinked at the sight of the burned body. It looked so small like a child's. She heard the guide question the men. The same man said, "She hadn't touched her food for three days now, sir. You know what that means. So we were ordered to burn down her hut before the body gets eaten by rats. That's the law, sir. You don't want contamination in the hamlet."

"She was still alive," the guide said.

"She could be," the man said.

When the guide turned to her, she felt lightheaded. She heard him ask gently if she could make her way back and she nodded. Then she closed her eyes. In them the blue-red flames danced, the tall bamboos spiraled in smoky gold.

The Red Fox

The boy went down the gravel path. The sea murmured far away and the salt-laden air was moist. Coming down the slope he could see the sky low over the sea now gone dark the color of eggplant. He could smell a strong, musky smell. A red fox slunk away among the tall grass and disappeared behind a clump of bushwillows. In the dying sunlight its fur was of the fire. He watched it saunter up and down the rise and fall of sand dunes toward the distant lighthouse. He hoped it was wise enough to stay away from the neighborhoods along the main road that circled the hill. Sometimes they set traps to catch the foxes that came in the night to steal their fowl.

*

When dawn came long after the tide had ebbed, the sand now dark and damp glistened at first light.

A red fox stood in the dune, raising its head toward the old lighthouse, and barked dryly. It saw the keeper sitting in a chair outside the door, a white-haired old man who smoked a long curving pipe. Across a patch of goat's foot vine the fox trotted on, its golden-furred body the only thing that moved in the morning-still heat. Coming out of the grass and across the brow of the dune among sprawling shrubs of sea grapes, it stopped and lowered its muzzle to sniff a gopher tortoise. After a while it lost interest and looked around. Then it moved on up the foredune making a small furtive shadow in the sand, past clumps of pitcher's thistles, out in the sun now among sandreed grasses, leaving behind its star-shaped footprints in the sand.

The fox stopped on the wooden steps that led up to the keeper's house, a tin-roofed abode built of wood that sat beside the yellow-painted lighthouse. The old man reached down in a brass pail at his feet, picked up a bluefish and tossed it down the steps. He drew on the pipe, watching the fox work over the fish with its paws and muzzle. Its golden pelt shone in the sun. Across its shoulders and down the center of its back were cross-stripes the color of rusty red. By the time the old man finished his pipe and now repacked it with fresh tobacco, the fox had also eaten its meal, leaving just bones on the steps. The old man threw it another bluefish, wiped his hand on his trousers, and lit his pipe. When he looked up through the curling smoke, he saw a boy standing hunched up with a backpack, on the flat ground to one side of the house. The boy raised his hand to greet and the old man took the pipe out of his mouth.

"Hey there," the old man said.

"Morning, sir."

The fox paused in its eating and regarded the boy. Its black eyes glittered in the sun.

"Some fox," the boy said. "He knows where to get his meal, eh?"

"Yep. Comes here for his fish just about this time rain or shine."

"Whew. Look at that coat."

"Aint it pretty?" The old man shifted in his rickety cane chair. "Told him to keep out of those damn hunters around here. Treasure to em if they skin him."

"Well, only if they figure out his routine."

"He can take care of himself. He knows, cause he's a fox."

The boy nodded at the old man's laugh that sounded like a snort. "You know where he might come from, sir?"

"Yonder in the backdunes."

"I saw him last night when I went down to the beach. I think it's him."

The old man, laying the pipe in his lap, said sometimes in the early morning you could see its tracks in the sand and, if you follow them, you could tell about its habitual itinerary.

"How can you tell if they're his footprints and not a dog's footprints?" The boy glanced toward the old man and back at the fox.

"How? They have two toes, two claws in front just like dog's footprints. Difference is he leaves his prints in a pair of straight line. Always overlapping. Dogs leave four prints 'cause they get excited outdoors and they run wild." The keeper paused to take a deep drag on his pipe. "Where're you from, son?"

"Not from here, sir. I'm looking for work. They said the foreman's out to sea."

"Two, three days usually." The old man spat at his feet and wiped his lips and white moustache. "The fishing boats are due back today."

The boy watched the fox hold the remains of bones in its jaw and set off toward the backdunes. He wondered what it planned to do with the fishbones.

The old man, scratching his bearded leathery face, pointed in the fox's direction and said, "There he goes. Always polite to dump the crap somewhere else but here." He held the pipe out in front of him and nodded at the boy. "Come on up. Rest your bones."

The boy hitched up the backpack and crossed the ground to the narrow porch. He stood, massaging his shoulders, trailing his gaze across the vast foredunes as far as the distant hamlet that sat back from the curve of the sand line.

"That looks like another world over there," the boy said, lifting his chin toward the hamlet.

"Just three kilometers as the crow flies." The old man gazed out to the ocean. "So you been down there, son?"

"Yessir. Slept on the beach last night."

"Mosquitoes didn't carry you away, eh?"

"Nope. But the ghost crabs almost did." He told the old man how hundreds of thousands of them came down to the water and then retreated.

"They get oxygen from the water that way," the old man said. "That's how they survive. Around the time their eggs hatch, some nights you could hear the sand move out there. Sounds like shoveling. Make it thousands of shovels. And son, can those little things wreck the fishing nets."

The boy nodded, noticing a fishing net hung on an upright branch of a sea grape tree by the side of the house. The tree's multiple twisted trunks were surrounded by their own earthbound branches and their picturesque shape held the boy's gaze.

"You fish too, sir?" he said, turning his head toward the old man.

"Nah, son. Never been a fisherman in my life. I mend nets for 'em though. Around here when the season starts, they're too busy doing nothing else but fishing." The old man jabbed his pipe toward the hung net. "What takes time when you fix those nets is to re-crimp the lead points. Old nets you must dye 'em again sometimes. They last longer that way."

"I fixed nets. Haven't dyed none of 'em though. Didn't have the time like you."

"That's all I been doing, son. Ever since I been here."

"I'm not gonna ask how long ago," the boy said, grinning.

"Forty some years. Operating this lighthouse and doing odd jobs for 'em fishermen."

The boy shook his head and sat down on the backpack. "Have you got a family, sir?"

"Everyone has a family, son," the old man said, fingering his drooping moustache. "Then one by one they all departed. Whew. This lighthouse is older than me and it'll be here still standing when I come back in my next life. Believe that."

"Yessir."

The old man was gazing out to the sea now a bluish gray as far as the horizon and the gray turned darker closer to shore. The sea heaved and the breakers foamed white.

"All these years," the old man spoke quietly. "She'd have been older than you."

"What sir?"

The old man seemed lost in his thought. He held the pipe at his lips but didn't light it. "All these years," he said.

"Who were you talking about?"

The old man puffed deeply, filling his lungs, and exhaled two streams of smoke out of his nostrils. "By the time she turned fifteen, she'd read all the books in the town's library." He paused to take a deep drag from his pipe. "I just fix nets. She made nets. Dandy kind. She was a fifteen-year-old going twenty that's how ripe she was."

"Where's she now?" the boy's voice was exasperated.

"Every morning I sit out there watching the sun come up. Know what I think? Think if I keep sitting there with my hope day after day, I might just see her. Coming back in one of 'em boats that came here on one of those nights. Thoughts are things, they said. Hellfire.

So if I keep thinking of her, she might just appear. Had this dream here. Came to me just once. She came to me as a fox. Might be a red fox. Licked my hand and I woke up. Ain't it strange?"

The boy looked at the old man whose sun-browned face was grooved with deep lines and full of sunspots. A gash ran from his jawline down the side of his neck to where his collarbones were. Now he raised the pipe to his lips, his heavy-lidded eyes narrowed at something in front of him that only he himself saw in his head.

"What happened to her?" the boy said.

The old man puffed on the pipe, his forefinger tapping down the glowing tobacco. "Was a night, rainy night," he said, smoke curling up out of the corners of his mouth. "Their boats came to the beach in pitch dark. Raided the hamlet, went house to house, dragged out every girl her age, bar none. Then went to the lighthouse. Took her. I threw myself at 'em. One of 'em cut me down with a knife." The old man touched the scar on the side of his neck. "Crawled from here to there, he said, motioning with his chin lifted toward the door. Plugged the cut with my hand and sat there and felt blood run down my arm and drip to the floor. Sat and watched her gone, till I could watch no more."

"Who were they?"

"Khmer pirates."

"They ever come again after that?"

"No. Them fishermen built a stockade around the hamlet. Has watchtowers, guns. The work."

"Any of 'em kidnapped girls came back?"

The old man said nothing. The boy thought he was hard of hearing when the old man slowly shook his head. "Them girls," he said, "were sold into prostitution."

*

When morning came, a light rain was falling and the sea was rough. The winds raised enormous swells in the ocean, rolling in from long rips offshore, the white-crested waves coming in twenty-foot-tall walls that broke over rocky reefs, sending immense lips to crash ashore with thunderous sounds.

The boy, after spending the night in the keeper's house, came down to the beach and saw tracks in the sand. The footprints, shaped like apricot flowers, were neat in the wet sand. That fox was out here early, the boy thought as he followed the tracks where the fox's footmarks suddenly became erratic, gapped. Then he saw a hollow in the sand, yellowed like turmeric, peppered with blood-darkened spots. He squinted his eyes, puzzled. *I wonder what he killed? Or what happened to him?*

*

A large crowd of people huddled on the beach. Far out in the ocean wave after wave was foaming white, and the winds blew the foam up into a swirling mist.

The boy stood among the villagers. They gazed out to sea. On the sand, fishing boats lay resting on long, round levers, their oak hulls coated with copper liquid paint to protect against barnacles now dripping with seawater. They said seventeen boats made it back before daybreak, and one did not. Several of them had straggled till dawn and ran out of fuel and had to be rowed with oars. But one by one they came back, the men exhausted, many collapsing. Among those missing were the foreman and his crew. The men said they were completely cut off from one another in the tar-black night. Each boat was on its own hazardous journey, pounded by gale driven rain, tossed about by giant waves that knocked men overboard, at times spun like a leaf and completely disoriented in the blackness blacker than the Avichi Hell. The eight-mile trip back to shore lasted the whole night.

The boy stood listening to a middle-aged man, the deputy foreman, who told the crowd of his rescue plan. He needed a four-man crew, and he got two, counting himself. One man who had just barely made it home, still battered by the night-long ordeal, volunteered to head back out. A woman clung to the man's arm and wailed, "Please find my husband. You hear me, brother? You save him and the Buddha will tell you that's more than building ten pagodas."

The man, still drenched from the rain, looked spent. "We'll bring 'em back, sis," he said. "We will."

"We need another hand," the deputy foreman said to the crowd and the crowd looked at one another.

The volunteering man said to him, "I think we can man it with three."

"Not in this condition," the deputy foreman said. "And you know that."

The boy raised his hand and his voice, "I'll go with you."

"You?" the deputy foreman said, hooking his thumbs onto his belt. "I don't believe I've seen you before."

"Does it matter?" The boy hitched up the backpack on his shoulders. "You can use me. I know boats."

"You'd better do," the deputy foreman said and snapped his fingers at the other two men. "Fill her up and get her to sea."

As the men refueled the boat, the boy tossed his backpack into the transom and then walked around the weather-beaten boat, looking up at the owl's eyes painted on either side of the upswept prow. He knew man has to believe in something to put his mind at ease. So he believes in the eyes that help guide him home in foul weathers on high sea.

The crowd stood watching them roll the boat on the lever toward the water. As soon as it hit a breaker, the four of them jumped onto the boat, two at the prowl and two at the stern, each grabbing an oar steering the boat straight over the roaring waves. The boat dipped and rose like a cork, turning sideways at times and the men bent low, sculling it so its prow nosed into the wind. Soon it rode out beyond the rip and its motor now churned.

At the bow the deputy foreman sat up on one knee, watching the horizon through his binoculars.

*

It was late afternoon when they brought the boy in to the hamlet's infirmary so the doctor could look at his calf wound. He was feeling very low and thirsty from loss of blood. A shark had torn his lower leg. They had wrapped his wound tightly with a tourniquet to stay the flow of blood and, as soon as the rescue boat hit the shore with the crippled boat in tow, the foreman and three other men carried the boy up the flagstone path and took a split up the road. They laid him in the bed of the foreman's pickup truck and drove up the hill behind the dunes.

The old doctor sterilized his wound to prevent blood poisoning and then proceeded to inject several syringes of serum to stabilize his agonized condition. The foreman stayed with the doctor in the infirmary, watching the boy's blanched face for signs of recovery. Under sedation he was asleep while the doctor was stitching the tears on his calf. The foreman watched. The room was quiet, save the doctor's raspy breathing as he slowly sewed up each crescent-shaped tear rent by the shark's teeth. Parallel tears. In all his life as a fisherman, the foreman had seen worse of shark bites. Sometimes good chunks of flesh were ripped off and the wound diameters were so extensive the arm or leg had to be amputated. Yet the boy was fortunate when the shark had only locked on to his lower leg. His leg could have been mutilated had the shark snapped its formidable jaw. To his dismal recollection, the foreman had brought shark victims to this doctor only to take them to the local hospital to have their limbs amputated and their lives saved.

Out of respect for the old doctor's work, the foreman kept quiet, also knowing the doctor's propensity for reticence. Hands clasping on the front of his stomach, he shifted his legs now and then, doing it surreptitiously so not to distract the doctor. At last, the doctor straightened his back, looking down over the rims of his glasses to survey the work just done. Then he pushed the glasses up with his middle finger, holding the long needle between his thumb and forefinger away from his sunken cheek.

"Let him stay here for a few days," the doctor spoke to the foreman without looking back at him. "You know the drill."

"Yes, doc."

"Have you told his family?"

"His family?" The foreman cracked his knuckles. "I don't even know who he is."

"Precisely you mean that he's not from the hamlet, is he?"

"No, doc. My deputy told me he just volunteered for the

rescue." The foreman swallowed. "He saved me from the shark. One that got him good."

"I only treat folks from the hamlet. If they're not from there, take them to the county clinic."

The foreman reached his hand into his trousers' side pocket, missed, and balled up his fist. "You're right, doc. I shoulda done that. I just took him here as quickly as I could. Coulda gone to town. But then the distance, the wait there. He coulda been in jeopardy. You know what I mean, doc."

The old physician, saying nothing, put away the needle and raised himself up on his creaky knees. The foreman scratched the side of his mouth. "He's a good boy," he spoke to the doctor's back, who nodded.

"If there're no signs of infection within twenty-four hours," the doctor spoke over his shoulder, "he will be out of danger." He paused then said, "But not out of pain."

"I'll bring him a pair of crutches. Got a few lying around."

*

When they got inside the keeper's house the old man shut the door, took off his raincoat and hung it on a metal hook behind the door. The boy, leaning his crutches against the wall, heard the wind coming over the tin roof, feeling it shake.

All he saw were a square wooden table with two ladderback chairs in one corner, bowls turned upside down on the table, a paper wrapped bundle as long as a baguette next to a familiar jar of rice liquor near empty. The walls painted ocher-yellow were a shade darker than the yellow on the lighthouse. Between the two shuttered windows he could see the spines of old books that filled the three wooden shelves. Suddenly he felt awed. The lighthouse's beam sweeping across the night's blackness shone through the gaps in the shutters' slats. The sound of waves pounding the shore. The shutters shook. He felt the wind in the room, a salted air that it brought.

The old man was nursing a fire in the coal brazier, sitting on his haunches, one hand still clasping the rice liquor jar. The boy sat down across from the old man, watching him unwrap the paper bundle and place two sundried ribbonfish on the brazier. The boy thought they looked like silver eels with blade-like bodies and mean-looking heads. The old man turned over the elongate fish, the skins now blistering and a thick fatty odor rising. He poured liquor into the two bowls.

"Been a while since I drank with somebody," the old man said.

"Since when?"

"It ain't like since yesterday," the old man said as he turned the fish again. "On nights like this here I have to get up to check on that light up there, to make sure we got light in case somebody who got lost on high sea could see it all right."

"Thanks, sir." The boy chuckled. "I'm damn sure glad you remembered me and hauled my ass back here in the middle of the night."

"Otherwise, I'd just sit here and listen to the waves and the winds and 'em night birds. Some nights just drink and mend the nets. Best way to kill time, son."

They drank and tore the dried fish with their fingers and ate. The boy let the flavor cut through his taste buds and took a sip of the liquor to wash it down. "Pffff," he said. "Where you got this fish from?"

"Caught'm myself. We had gales a couple weeks ago. Pushed 'em to shore. Them fish live in deep waters and you rarely see 'em."

They drank up their bowls and what remained in the jar. The old man fetched another jar and heated it over the coals. Then they drank down two more bowls and ate all the dried fish. The boy, watching the old man make a fresh pipe, said, "What're 'em books you got up there?"

"Chinese classics," the old man said and went on to light his pipe by holding against the bowl an ember with a pair of chopsticks.

"You read 'em all?"

"Over and over. You read?"

"No, sir. I ain't much for the learned stuff."

"Man gotta read. It wakes up the man in the child and child in the man."

The boy fixed his gaze on a framed drawing hung on the bare

wall. He recognized the red fox. "Did you draw that thing, sir?"

"Doodling when I ain't got nothing else to do."

"Looks just like him." The boy sipped from the bowl of liquor. It had been two weeks since he was mauled in the leg by the shark. But now seeing the fox in the drawing got him remembering what he saw that morning on the beach. "I came upon his footprints before I went out on that rescue mission. Saw something else, too."

"Something else what?" The keeper's face had a dark scowl.

The boy described the yellowed depression, the bloodlike spots in the sand.

The keeper's gaze fell on the framed drawing. A trancelike look passed on his face while the pipe smoldered in his lap. After a while he said, "That fox ain't around no more."

"He ain't? Why?"

"They killed him."

"Who?"

"Those from the hamlet. They'd figured out his run and set a trap."

"What kind of trap?"

"They knew what foxes like to eat. So they used pieces of chicken skin and wrap each of 'em around a wad of sulfur and metal bits. They put 'em charges in a cage and set it on the dune where they knew that fox would come by."

"The yellow stuff I saw was sulfur?"

"Used for explosive." The old man cycled his jaw on the stem of his pipe, his eyes turned beady as if in his mind he saw the moment the fox fell for the men's deception. "When that fox snapped up a chicken-skin ball, the charge blew up his snout, blinded his eyes."

The boy held the liquor in his mouth then slowly gulped it. The old man poured himself another bowl of liquor and took the pipe from his mouth. His scratchy voice dropped to a whisper. "When I brought them their repaired nets, they showed me his pelt. The red in his fur looked so real like he was still sitting out there waiting for me to throw him a bluefish."

*

The sea was calm and high tide was coming. The boy went down the slope in front the lighthouse through a patch of goat's foot vine. He found his footing along the rocky shore and down the slope screened with tall sea oats, walking between clumps of prickly pear cactus and saw palmetto till he reached the level ground beneath the lighthouse. Wolf spiders were now coming out of their burrows in the sand. He watched them push out the tiny pebbles they plugged their holes with against floodwater.

Leaning on his crutches, he looked up to the tin-roofed house where the keeper lived. He saw the cane chair where the old man would sit at first light waiting for the fox to come for his fish. He thought of the story the old man told him. That his daughter once came to him as a fox.

There was no light inside. The boy stood, remembering the red fox.

The General Is Sleeping

She was rail thin and tall. After three days lying in the same hospital bed, I could tell upon waking that she had been in the room while I was sleeping. An unmistakable musk in the air came from her body. A fragrance perhaps.

Coming out of sedation for the first time, I had felt clean below. Someone must have washed me.

I was clad only in a hospital gown. My right leg was suspended in a contraption, a pulley and a horizontal metal rod overhead. The leg seemed to have a life of its own, after having been crushed in a head-on collision between my car and a drunk driver's.

On the second day when the pain became bad, they gave me medication for it. I woke, feeling as if the pillow were a giant beanbag, feeling very cool between the legs from a moist antiseptic tissue.

The rubbing. I decided to be asleep while I was being cleaned there. I heard the rustle of a gown and then felt the warmth of a washcloth pressed against my face. I smelled her musk scent.

I opened my eyes.

A golden-brown face was looking down at me. The long-lashed eyes gleamed. The smile revealed dazzlingly white teeth.

"Ah, you're awake now." Holding the washcloth, she watched me.

I said a hello, but I couldn't hear the word I spoke for the drumming in my head. I felt drugged.

She stooped to look me full in the face. "How are you this evening, Mr. Lee?" She spoke with an accent.

"*Leh*," I said. "Not Lee." I spelled it for her. LE.

"Ah, Mr. Leigh. I'm Aida."

I was amused at how she pronounced my last name, the small tongue roll with the L.

She dabbed my stitched forehead with the washcloth. The musk aroma went with her hand. Her oval face was delicate. She was in her twenties, perhaps. Her cornrows were knotted into a thick plait, slung over her shoulder onto her chest.

"I'll bring your dinner, Mr. Leigh." She straightened.

Tall in her blue uniform. If I were to stand next to her, my head would be to her ears.

"Where are you from?" I asked, squinting.

"I'm from Senegal."

"Do you speak French?"

"Yes. Do you, Mr. Leigh?"

"A little. My father spoke French fluently."

"Ah. It brightens my day whenever I hear someone speak French." Her clear voice had a resonance. Then, frowning, she leaned her head to one side. "You have received no visitors since you're here?"

"My father died some years ago."

"What about your mother, Mr. Leigh?"

"She died shortly after my father's death, and I have no siblings."

Aida folded the washcloth. "Are you married, Mr. Leigh?"

"I was once."

"Did she know about your accident?"

"No. And even if she did . . ."

My voice was curt, and Aida dipped her head. "You sound like you have something against her?"

"She hated my family," I blurted out.

"How come?"

"In fact, she hated my father."

"Why?"

My chest heaved. "My father and my mother did not attend our wedding. It embarrassed me, but it humiliated my wife. My ex-wife. If there's one person in this world she hated most, it's my father."

"I don't assume that your father was a terrible man."

"Thank you." I nodded at her gentle smile. I still felt self-conscious that she was the one who had been cleaning my body.

"So, what happened?"

"My wife—my ex-wife—had never told me about her own family, though she knew much about mine. When we decided to get married, she told me about her father. He used to be a celebrated musician in South Vietnam. Millions of fans idolized him. To me, he was a gentleman, and I liked him. Then, I brought the news of our engagement home to my father, and hell broke out."

Aida blinked. She had dense lashes with a dramatic upsweep.

Her longish eyes were God-made beauty.

"My father told me, 'That scumbag is a Communist. He lives right in our backyard, and we can't do nothing about it.' I said, 'How do you know?' and he said, 'He's a mole. We have many moles and termites like him in our army too. We executed several of them, but we couldn't touch a man of his stature.'"

"This was back in Vietnam during the war, Mr. Leigh? You and she . . ."

"No, after we came to America. We met here, but our past never died. I mean her father's past."

"And what did your father do during the war?"

"My father was a general, a four-star general of the Army of the Republic of Vietnam."

"Ah. So he was a big shot." She squinted her eyes. "It must have been very difficult for him to leave Vietnam and come here."

"It was."

"For a man of his position, I'm sure." She put the washcloth into her blouse pocket. "What did he do in this country, Mr. Leigh?"

"He drove a forklift." I paused. "From five to midnight. Every night."

"I guess nobody around your father knew who that forklift operator really was." She smiled with a slight nod. "Yes?"

"Yes, just an old Asian man who came to work every night with a dinner box his wife packed for him. Every night for nine years."

"Then what, Mr. Leigh?"

"Then his kidneys started failing. He had diabetes. Eventually," I kept nodding to the unfinished sentence, "he lost a leg to amputation, and from there he went downhill fast."

We both glanced at my leg in the stirrup.

Aida went around the bed to the other side to check on the urinary catheter. "You need to drink more," she said, dropping my gown down. "You still think a lot about your ex-wife, yes?"

I held her gaze, until she blinked. Those almond-shaped eyes made my heart go soft. "Yes," I said.

"What about her?"

I tried to smile.

It must have looked like a grimace to her, for she took my hand in hers, held it and said, "You have nice hands, Mr. Leigh. Like my people's."

She opened her hand, the fingers long and tapered with symmetrical nails. "Let me get your dinner. Are you hungry, Mr. Leigh?"

*

My hands shook, so she fed me.

I didn't have a brain injury, but besides the gash on my forehead and my shattered shinbone, I must have had a mild concussion. At least I knew that much after a series of tests. This explained why my hands trembled, when I tried to feed myself.

I wasn't feeling hungry, only numb in my lower leg. In time the dullness would give way to pangs that my brain remembered well.

Aida placed the tray on its legs over my lap; the food smelled warm, unappetizing.

"Do you like lentil soup, Mr. Leigh?" she asked, as she lowered the bed and sat down on a chair.

"I like clam chowder."

"I'll check with the kitchen the next time." She spoon-fed me.

My tongue felt like rubber, and not until the bowl was near empty did I begin to register an aftertaste of lentil. I watched her slicing through the golden breaded chicken cutlet.

"I knew this man," I said to her, "a male nurse who took care of my father, when he was confined to a nursing home." Aida fed me a piece of chicken, her lips slightly parted as I opened my mouth. "He was like you, a Senegalese."

"Really." She spooned some mashed potato, and I ate that. Then, she pierced a baby carrot with the fork and held it until I opened my mouth again. "What's his name?"

"Ibou." I chewed the soft baby carrot. I liked carrots, and their familiar smell suddenly made me feel homesick.

She fed me another slice of chicken. "Was he also young like me?"

"No. He was a senior nurse." I swallowed and sighed. "He loved to speak French with my father."

"*C'est beau.*"

"He found out that my father was once a four-star general, that he was a Viet Minh who fought the French during the Indochina

War. Ibou told my father that his own father was with the French Foreign Legion that fought in Dien Bien Phu in 1954, a decorated soldier who lost a leg during the siege. Ibou joked with my father—Wouldn't it be extraordinary if it was my father who had set the trap that claimed his father's leg?"

Aida's lips parted. Then, she smiled.

She had a perfectly shaped upper lip; her full lower lip pouted when she did not smile.

"You two must be of the same age, yes?" she said.

"I'm thirty-six. I couldn't tell exactly how old he was."

"We Senegalese do look younger than we are, just like the Asians." She tilted her head, as if to avoid my gaze. "Did he make an impression on you?"

"He was always polite. I remember his accent—like yours. He was some kind of a rare species."

Her eyes opened wide, lips puckered. "How do you mean, Mr. Leigh?"

"He must have been at least seven feet tall." I looked toward the door and back at her. "Whenever he entered the room, he had to lower his head. Have you seen anyone like that back home?"

"Tall men? Yes, but not that tall." She offered me a gulp of chocolate milk, and I gladly obliged, for she'd told me that I ought to drink more. "Did you get along with him like your father did?"

"Yes, Ibou was a gentleman."

She was about to feed me another slice of chicken, but I held up a hand. "I'm full."

She peeled the lid off of a cup of red Jell-O.

While its raspberry flavor burst in my mouth, she pinched a flake of gelatin off my lips. Her musk fragrance mixed with the raspberry.

"So he took care of your father?" she said. "For how long?"

"Two years. Until my father died." I dropped my gaze to her hand. "He used to change my father's clothes all by himself. Before Ibou, it took two female nurses to do that chore. My father's imbalance after losing the leg made it harder to change him out of his clothes or to dress him, but Ibou did that chore so effortlessly that he became my father's sole caretaker."

"You were married then?" She paused with the spoon in midair.

"Yes, but my wife never visited my father."

"Your ex-wife must be beautiful, yes?"

"To me."

"And you must have had lots of girls before you met her?" As she brought the spoon to my mouth, her little finger touched my lips. At my smile, she tipped her head back. "Short girls, tall girls. Americans, Asians. Yes?"

I chuckled, shaking my head.

She said, "How tall are you, Mr. Leigh?"

"Five-seven." I nodded at her. "And you?"

"Five-eleven."

"You don't need high heels, ever."

"I don't look right in them, I'm sure."

"You're long-legged, like those Vogue girls, except they're on spike heels."

"Those million-dollar girls." Aida shook her head, her eyes trailing away. "I don't look anything like them."

"No, you don't." I saw a startled look in her eyes. "You look plain and beautiful—the way you are."

Her eyes flinched, then became soft. I thought I saw a blush on her cheeks, for the first time.

"I used to be self-conscious about my skin," she said, "because my mother told me how life was when she grew up in the colonial time. Black skin was despised, forbidden to mix with white society without permission. Growing up, my mother was an educated and beautiful girl, and yet she dreaded the color of own skin so much that she wanted to cover her arms and neck, to put on a big straw hat with a veil to hide her face. Age gave her maturity. She did not want me to suffer the same identity crisis, though she still feared that someday I might have *mulatto* children. She took me to social events, where I performed our *sabar* dance, to express myself in the free form of footwork and arm movements. She made me aware of such words as *nègres* and *négresses*, telling me that the word *noir* for black ceased to exist after the 1791 massacres in Santo Domingo."

Aida paused. Her large, gleaming eyes held me with a gentle smile. "Do you know about the Santo Domingo massacres?"

"No," I said, feeling ignorant.

She went on to give me a brief history of the slave revolt in the

French colony of Santo Domingo that led to the expulsion of the French colonial government and, hence, the establishment of the independent Republic of Haiti.

She put down the empty Jell-O cup and smiled. "Here," she said, picking up one of the two cookies. "I threw these in. They only give you one kind of dessert."

"Jell-O and cookies." I took a small bite of one cookie and then picked up the other for her. "Please, try it, if you like. Cinnamon cookie."

She nibbled at it. I watched her drooping eyelids. Those thick lashes with their beautiful curl didn't need mascara.

She looked up. "What do you do, Mr. Leigh?"

"Call me Minh."

"*Min?*" She made a humming sound with the M.

I reached for the glass of milk. "I'm a photographer."

"So you take pictures? Of what?" She looked at me with a spark in her eyes.

"I shoot advertising photography, for printed catalogs. Things that you browse before you decide to buy."

"Not fashion photography?" she said with a trailing smile.

"Just an old-fashioned photography business. No fashion models or nude girls."

Her fluty laugh sounded girlish. She tossed her head back, and her hair plait swung behind the nape of her neck. For the first time I noticed her elegant and slender neck, framed by the round neckline.

"Were you close to your father, Mr. Leigh?"

"Minh." I put the last piece of cookie into my mouth. "I was not."

"Ah. But you love him, don't you, Min?"

I said nothing. Then, I nodded. "It took me all my life to feel that—after he died."

"In his condition, he must have looked to you for care." She tore open the packet of sanitizer and gave me one wet tissue. "I'm very close to my mother. She almost died giving birth to me, but God saved her and me," she said.

"Where is she now?"

"Back home. With my father." Aida covered the meal plate with its lid. "My father was struck with a viral disease once. He bled in his bowels and in his nose, and there was blood in his urine. Hemorrhagic fever. We were with him all the time during his illness, because he needed us. He cried when he was alone, for it made him think Death was waiting for that rare moment to take him away in his sleep."

I cleaned my mouth with the wet wipe. I couldn't help remembering the sanitizing smell that hung in the room, whenever she cleaned my body as I slept. "My father was different," I said to her. "He really was."

"He didn't need you? I mean, we all need love and care." Slowly, she folded my tissue into quarters. "Maybe, he didn't want to show you his tender side, yes?"

"To the best of my recollection, I can't say that he was an affectionate father. Maybe I was insensitive to what he might've needed from me."

*

No, I never felt close to my father.

I told Aida about incidents during my boyhood, how when I did something terribly wrong, he would lash me. To keep count, he had our chauffeur, a corporal, call out each lash. One. Two. Three. Four. To this day, I still heard the counting sound.

I had thought of him often after the car accident. Now, I thought of him, while the doctor made a thorough evaluation of my shattered leg, while an orderly wheeled me back to my room.

Could my leg be saved? The doctor would tell me soon. It was evening. I had not eaten dinner.

Through the window I could see a full moon. I didn't feel pain in the leg, at least for now. I wouldn't until the pain killer wore off.

Closing my eyes to rest, I smelled the familiar musk in the room. She must have been here, while I was taken to the examination room.

A female nurse brought in my dinner tray.

"Can you eat by yourself?" she said, as she placed the tray over my lap.

"Sure." I pushed the control to raise the adjustable head section.

"If you need anything else, please ring." She glanced at my leg suspended in midair. "You have any pain, Mr. Lee?"

"Not at this moment." I slid up on the bed. "Where's Aida?"

"She's on her rounds. We have a new patient."

I ate only after the nurse left. My hands still shook, so I concentrated on each movement. I sipped some apple juice, looking at the tray. It held baked salmon, mashed potatoes, peas, and carrots. There was also a bowl of chicken noodle soup and a slice of chocolate cake for dessert.

I took a deep breath. Sometime tonight, the doctor would come in and tell me the news.

My father had looked calm on the day he'd had his leg amputated above the knee. If I hadn't lifted his gown to look at what then resembled a stump, I would have sworn it was any other day to him. He didn't mention the surgery that day, though he asked me the next time to come in with my mother. "Do not let her drive," he said. "Her nerves are very fragile, now."

Later, Ibou told me something that has haunted me since. "The general did not remember," Ibou said, always referring to my father with that title. "This is common, after you wake up from a surgery. When I changed him, he pulled up his legs, and, trust me, Mr. Leh, a thousand words could not describe that look in his eyes. The general recovered quickly, though. I don't mean physical recovery. A moment later, the general began to chat with me in French. *Oh-la-la.*" Ibou laughed heartily. "He told me things."

"What things?" I asked.

Ibou said, "Fragments of his life as a boy and as a soldier. Fascinating. One day I asked him if he could read them into a cassette for me, and he said, '*Bien sûr, mon ami.*'

"So I brought in a mini-cassette recorder, and during his undisturbed moments he spoke those stories into the recorder. When he gave me the whole thing back, he asked me, '*Pourquoi voulez-vous de garder ces histoires?*'

"I told him, 'General, I'm a writer.'

"'*Un écrivain?*' he said. '*C'est très noble.*'

"One story I couldn't shake off took place in the summer of 1972. He called that summer the Blazing Summer—the Vietnam War was at its worst. That summer, the Vietnamese marines recaptured Quang Tri Province. From Hue, a convoy was dispatched to Quang Tri to relieve the marines and to reinstall the former administration. Escorted back to the city were the exiled province chief and his entourage. Local merchants and residents tagged along behind the convoy, to return home. The general was one of them."

Ibou shook a finger as if to warn me not to ask questions. I did not.

He continued. "The convoy had to cross a bridge. Just as it approached the bridgehead, shelling exploded. From a nearby mountain the Viet Cong was firing mortars. The mile-long convoy was broken up. After many rounds of shelling, the Viet Cong failed to hit the bridge.

"Suddenly, all eyes fell upon an old woman who appeared out of nowhere. She was carrying two cane baskets suspended from a shoulder pole. In one was her clothing, in the other a little boy. The shelling had trapped her in the middle of the bridge. She froze.

"No one from the convoy dared leave his cover, but the general jumped up and raced toward her. He carried the boy and half-carried the old woman back to the roadside shelter.

"Within minutes, air support came. Soon, the convoy got rolling again."

Ibou put his hand on my shoulder. "Now, you may ask why the general disguised himself as a commoner. *Très bien.* He disguised himself, so he could assess the morale of the troops and the civilians, and to take in firsthand the damages to the city against possible false reports."

*

I told Aida the story.

When she entered the room, I was resting, half-reclined with the dinner tray on my lap, the meal unfinished, my eyes closed. The musk scent woke me from my reflection.

I noticed the cardinal-red ribbon that adorned her usually plain plait. I couldn't help saying, "It looks pretty on you, Aida."

"Thank you, Min," she said, looking down at me and then at my dinner.

"Where were you?" I already knew the answer, but I still wanted to hear it from her.

"I was in here earlier. You were being examined, so I went to where they needed me." She touched the cup of chicken noodle soup, still lidded. "It's getting warm. Do you want me to reheat it, Min?"

"Don't bother. Do you have to go soon?"

"No, I'm on my break." Glancing at the meal, she said, "Let me see if you can eat by yourself."

I removed the lid of the soup cup, while she watched. I was distracted by the musk scent, and my hand started trembling.

She deftly pressed the control button, so that the bed dropped, whirring. She sat down on the chair and took the cup from my hand.

"You're on your break, Aida," I said meekly.

"That's why I'm here." She held her smile as she brought the spoon to my lips.

Taking her time between spoonfuls, she asked me about the examination.

I told her that within an hour or two I would know. "Know what they will do with your leg?" she said casting a glance at my suspended leg.

Sighing, I nodded.

"You didn't want to eat. You must be worried, yes?"

"I'm fine." I lied.

"You should pray, Min. It will take the worries and fears off your mind."

"I don't see how." My throat felt dry despite the soup. "I never believed in prayer."

"My father said that it's belief, faith, that keeps men in touch with the supernatural beyond the praying and the worshiping. He said men are ignorant enough to think they can get along by themselves and that nothing they can't see or own matters." She put the cup down, took my hand, and held it between hers. "Just open your mind and pray, Min."

I bit my lips at the earnest look in her eyes and nodded like a simpleton.

My father had derided priests and monks. When my mother asked him, during a moment of his lucidity, if she could have a religious rite for his funeral, my father smirked. "Them priests and monks," he said. "Their spiritual lives are nothing but the empty sounds of recitation and chanting. Without a pagoda, without a church, what'd have become of their spiritual lives? Eh?"

I couldn't say whether or not he had sowed that notion of distrust in my mind.

Aida looked lost in thought. Then, she said, "Min, I'll pray for you, so you won't end up like your father. You never asked him much about his life, no?"

"No, I'd never asked him anything. Maybe someday I'd read somebody else's stories about him. That's my dad, I'd say."

"And Ibou would be the author?"

We both laughed. Aida canted her head to look at me. "Who do you look like? Your mother or your father?"

"My mother. I have no resemblance to my father."

"You sound like you deny it," she said, smiling.

I gaze at her lips, and she blushed.

"In her younger days," I said, "my mother had the kind of beauty that you'd call classic. I wonder what made her fall in love with my father." I cut the chocolate cake in half, lifted a piece with a napkin, and pushed the other piece on the plate toward her. "Please, share it with me."

She forked a piece, and I noticed that she was left-handed. "Your father must've adored your mother," she said before taking a bite.

"He was unfaithful to her," I said, before I'd thought it through. "She told me so, after he'd become an invalid. I guess she'd bottled it up all her life.

"She must have been upset with the way he perked up when he was with Ibou, becoming suddenly animated and carrying on and on in their small talks, in French, of course.

"When she was with him, he'd clam up. Most patients, I noticed, couldn't wait to see their loved ones. It's dreary and downright lonesome for most of them, but he didn't need her, his wife."

Aida sat riveted, nibbling her lower lip. "How did he . . . betray her?"

"Women have uncanny instincts. Don't you agree?" I asked. Her eyes glinted with amusement, as she nodded.

"I didn't ask my mother what triggered her suspicion, but at one point she told our chauffeur, the corporal, to report to her every place he drove my father. You see, my mother was the godmother of our chauffeur's little daughter, so he was loyal to her.

"He told her that every day around noon he dropped my father off in downtown Saigon, where he'd spend an hour or two in a pharmacy. One day, after dropping my father off at the usual place, our chauffeur came back and drove my mother to that place.

"My mother waited in the car, while it was parked outside the pharmacy, until my father came out. When he got into the car, her presence shocked the daylight out of him. She asked him to wait. Then, she went into the pharmacy. Fifteen minutes later she came back out, got into the car, and told the chauffeur to drive home.

"From that day on, my father quit going to visit his mistress."

"His mistress?" Aida's eyes widened.

"You wonder how my mother found out? She happened to go through his wallet one day and saw a picture of a woman. Yes, someone else's photo besides hers in his wallet. How foolish of him to keep his woman's picture, but I guess we're all blind when we're in love, aren't we?" I shook my head.

Aida chuckled. Her eyes looked dreamy. "It must've shocked your mother deeply when she saw the photograph of your father's mistress. I would be shocked too, if something of that nature happened to me."

"It tore her to pieces. She could never have imagined such a horrible thing. A man of his stature? A man who was so madly in love with her when they first met that he kept count of the days being away from her by marking a cut with a nail on his rifle's buttstock? You know what my mother did when she came upon the woman's picture?"

I met Aida's eyes. She hadn't touched the rest of her cake. "She cut it up and left the pieces in his wallet, this picture of his courtesan."

Aida giggled. "I like that word."

"That's the word my mother used when she told me the story. I thought she used this word, because my father was a man of rank, like a king at that time."

"Do you have any love for him, Min?"

"I've thought of him a lot since he died. My father is a good man."

"Of course."

"He never impressed me as a loving father, but he had a heart of gold. I knew this from an incident."

"Another incident? Back home?"

"No, here." I offered her my glass of apple juice, and she took it. "I was working at this advertising agency—my first job out of college. One late afternoon just before I left my cubicle, I saw an Asian woman, a janitor. She was in her fifties. She must've been in earlier than usual, because I'd never seen her before. She was dusting each cubicle, probably waiting for everyone to leave before vacuuming the floor. She didn't make a sound.

"When she reached my cubicle, I sensed her standing behind my chair. I decided to keep busy. When I finally turned around, she was still standing there. She gestured with her duster toward a framed picture on my desk.

"'Is that your father?' she asked in plain Vietnamese.

"I said, 'Yes.'

"In that picture, I was about five years old, sitting between my mother and my father.

"The cleaning woman took a step closer to my desk and said, 'He was in jail in 1961, right, Mister?'

"Something knifed my gut. I nodded. He had been in the prison of what used to be the Lê Loi artillery barracks, after the military *coup d'etat*, which had been carried out to overthrow President Diem, failed. My father, then a major general, was sentenced to life. That much I knew from my mother.

"The woman's gaze never left the framed picture on my desk, and I grew irritated.

"'Thank Heaven and the Buddha,' she blurted. 'I knew it was him. I looked at his picture every night when I came in to clean, but I didn't know who to ask about it. Mister, I don't have many debts in my life but one. A debt I owe your father for the welfare of my family, and . . .'

"She stuttered. For a moment she looked like a jabbering mental patient. 'It had to do with my son . . .'

"'Your son?' I said to her. 'Where is he now?'

"'He's studying to become a doctor now, in California. This debt had to do with my son, when he was a few months old. In 1961, I was put into jail in Saigon by the government.'

"I looked at her, no longer irritated but intrigued. 'What did you do to be thrown in jail?'

"'They charged me with conspiracy of silence,' she said.

'It happened after my husband suddenly disappeared. I didn't know where he went, but I knew he was taken by the Viet Cong. This happened all the time in my village. The Viet Cong said they recruited you, but nobody could ever say no to them. I reported his disappearance to the local authorities. They questioned me and asked me to come back in a week. I came back the next week.

"'Where's your husband? Back yet?' they asked.

"'No,' he's still gone, 'I told them.' That's when they arrested me.

"They said, 'We know where he went. Tell us where to find his base.'

"I couldn't tell them anything. How could I?

"They drove me and my four-month-old baby to Saigon and put us into the police headquarters' jail. In that courtyard, they took us to Ward B. That was the ward for Viet Cong. We were kept in Cell Number One, the only cell for females.'

"I kept my gaze on her, as she went on.

"'I was tortured every day. They forced me to drink soapy water 'til I became bloated. Then someone stepped on my stomach, and water came out of my mouth and my nose. The next day they jammed wires under my fingernails and turned on the current. My whole body jumped and went numb. I thought I'd lost all my limbs.

"'By the third day, my baby got sick. They had given us no blankets, though everyone else had them. It could be hot outside, but it was chilly inside—all the time. You know, Mister, there in damp cells, a blanket equals life. Without one, prisoners often caught pneumonia and died before receiving medical attention.'

"I stared at her. My body tensed up.

"She continued. 'My baby began having diarrhea. His cries kept everyone in the other cells awake at night. By the end of the first week, he'd lost so much body fluid that he became unconscious. I couldn't breast-feed him, anymore. I cradled him with what was left of me to keep him warm, but he was going away.

"'Someone from another cell gave up his own blanket for my baby. When they passed down the blanket, they said it was from Anh Ba—Brother Number Three. I heard that from that night on he slept on the floor, with a rush mat wrapped around him to keep warm. His blanket brought my baby back to life. The diarrhea stopped, and he was feeding again.

"'One month later, I was freed. When the warden let us out, I turned left instead of right for the exit.

"'You want to stay, woman?' the warden said.

"'No, sir,' I said, 'but allow me to thank Anh Ba.'

"'I went up to his cell. Cell Number Four, I remember to this day. There were three men in that cell. Anh Ba was a man in his early thirties. I put my baby down, prostrated myself in front of his cell, and kowtowed to him three times.

"'He waved me off, obviously embarrassed.

"'I said to him, 'Ân nhân—savior—my son and I will owe you this debt for the rest of our lives. I have nothing to give you in return, so please accept my three kowtows as my gratitude to you.' I wept in the silence of Ward B, as people in the other cells listened. Then I got up, bowed to him and left.'"

This was the janitor's story.

Aida handed me the glass of apple juice. "Your father is an unusual man," she said, with a note of admiration in her voice.

I nodded in agreement. One of the reasons I had talked at length with her because she knew how to listen. Then, there was something called compatibility. I had thought about that after my mother told me of my father's infidelity. Perhaps he found not only compatibility but also the fire that lit up his soul in his courtesan.

Entering the room was the nurse who'd brought my dinner. Aida said to her, "He's almost done. Let me take care of this."

"Sure," the nurse said. "Also, Doctor River will be here in half an hour to discuss the medical issue with Mr. Lee."

"Half an hour?" Aida and I looked at the wall clock. It was 9:30 p.m.

After the nurse left, Aida sat with her eyes on the floor. When she finally looked up, I saw a grim expression on her face. "Are you afraid, Min?"

"Perhaps," I said. In fact, I felt calm. Remembering my father and his indifferent attitude toward his own physical tragedy had given me the much-needed mettle.

"I'll be back at ten." Aida rose, lifting the tray from the bed. Her eyes, beautiful in their brooding, blinked as she bent and kissed me on the forehead.

"I'll go and pray for you."

*

She dimmed the light as she left.

I listened to the wall clock tick, as I lay looking at the ceiling. The leg didn't hurt, save the occasional throbbing.

What did Doctor River see, after he'd run the battery of tests earlier in the evening?

I wasn't there on the day the doctor told my mother and my father that—against the threat of gangrene—they had to amputate his right leg. The amputation, they always said, is to take a step toward improving the quality of your life.

When my mother and I visited him later in the nursing home, my father never talked about his handicap. If I mentioned his amputation, his answers were casual, as if he were talking about a missing slipper. When my mother and I left at the end of our visit, there was no gloominess about him. Sometimes, looking back toward him, I would see him turn his face toward the window and sleep.

What did he think of while he was awake, with all the time he had, lying in bed, or being wheeled outside for fresh air? I often wondered. Time must be painfully slow to pass for him, but then I wasn't him. I never had his mettle, his absence of self-pity.

One day, when I came into his room, he simply looked at me and smiled.

My mother said, "That's Minh."

He kept smiling, as if he and I never met. Only the sight of Ibou still stirred him up with excitement and brought back slivers of his memory.

After he died in the hospital, Ibou called me, asking how the general was doing. I told him.

I was in the hospital room, where my father lay with a white sheet covering his body, when Ibou came in.

He stood by the bed, looking down at my father for some time, then crossed himself.

"The general is sleeping," he said.

*

Now, I heard voices in the hallway. I could hear Doctor River's voice. I closed my eyes. They were still talking outside.

Then I smelled a musk scent. She was here.

All the Pretty Little Horses

Mama, I'm glad that you kept my oak bed. The little girl you brought home has slept on one side of the bed since she was five. Did she tell you the bed was too large? Now she's no longer a child, and I am twenty-three—I was twenty-two when I came to Vietnam and now my bones are buried somewhere in this godforsaken land. My bed fits her just right. Chi Lan. I can say her name with ease. But many Vietnamese names are harder to say.

I left America on September 25th, 1966, and have been in Nam twelve months and twenty days. Many of us here are my age or younger. We are young men in body but aged in the soul. Today we had a death in our company. His death took something away from me, Mama. Combat deaths often make me hollow inside and saddened.

I can't help thinking about the time I was two when you put me in that bed, first with Papa, then by myself. Papa told me he missed the closeness between father and son. So every night he would tuck me in, turn off the light, and lie down beside me. In the dark, Papa would tell me stories about growing up in Georgetown, a few alleys away from a Black neighborhood named Cherry Hill. People there had no indoor electricity or plumbing.

"The reason I'm telling you this," Papa said, "is so you'll remember that there's poverty in the world. There are people not nearly so fortunate as we are. I don't want you to take anything for granted. Your grandma worked sixty hours a week and took home a dozen shirts to sew on Sunday and earned a pittance. And the sweatshop owner still threatened to fire her and her friends and bring in the Chinese. The Chinese were willing to work for thirty dollars a month. She raised me, put me through college. A cup of coffee and a loaf of bread was all she ate the whole day, and she ate that every day of her working life."

"Why didn't she live with you and Mama?" I asked.

"Would've been too far for her. She thought she needed to work. Grandma was only fifty when she died."

"Did Grandma tell you stories at night when you were a child?"

"She was too tired by the time she got home."

"What happened to Grandpa?"

"He was a soldier. Then in June 1918, when I was just born, his outfit attacked the Germans in Belleau Wood to stop them from taking Paris, and he was killed."

*

I was in high school when Papa came back from Nam, though he never talked about it. I knew only what you told me—about his CIA service, and his time in the Green Berets before they came under the Military Assistance Command, Vietnam. I knew nothing about the MACV until I went to Officer Candidate School. They trained the Army of the Republic of Vietnam to defend South Vietnam against the Viet Cong and the North Vietnamese communists. Later on, I learned the MACV carried out a covert operation, Operation Phoenix—to neutralize Viet Cong suspects outside judicial controls, and kill every active Viet Cong cadre and South Vietnamese collaborator. He wasn't the same man, you said to me, after he came back. Mama, I can't recall what he was like before he left. He was a reticent man. Even with you, Mama. But he became even more distant. How quickly things fell apart for you and him. You were forty-one then, I remember.

*

One night I kept tossing and turning. Papa said, "What's wrong?"
"Why can't I sleep with Mama?"
"Mama goes to bed late."
"I don't mind."
Papa sighed. "She has insomnia. She needs rest."
You had insomnia, Mama, during your pregnancy. You could sleep only after a glass of wine. The insomnia got worse after the childbirth. You couldn't sleep at night. The piano you played downstairs would wake Papa in bed. *Go to sleep, baby child, Hush-a-bye, don't you cry. When you wake, you shall have, All the pretty little horses.*
Papa worried about biochemical imbalances in the brain. The doctors suggested a lamp with a bluish luminosity. Rainy days and wintry weather made Papa fret. Did she have enough light? Would she stay balanced? He grew accustomed to seeing the lamp glowing blue, and still there was too much darkness.

*

When I was a first grader, you and Papa wanted to put me in second grade. But the school didn't accommodate advanced students. The principal convinced you that the child still needed to develop social skills, because intelligence and maturity went hand in hand. The principal said she was pleased to have me in her school. Then, noting my bony legs, she mentioned the school's outstanding physical education program.

I rode the school bus every day. One evening Papa came home and found a note from the bus driver—it said I'd pushed a girl in the back on the bus steps. She scraped her knees and hands when she fell. She was the principal's daughter. Papa sat me down on the couch after dinner and asked me about the incident. I said the girl called me stupid.

"You must've done something to her," Papa said. "She wouldn't call you names for no reason."

"I didn't give her the seat she always sat in," I said. "She said it was her seat."

Papa squeezed my hand. "You don't push anyone in the back like that. It's uncalled for, it's dangerous."

"But I didn't push her. A kid behind me did."

"Nicola!" Papa glared at me. "Don't lie!"

"You don't trust me."

"I do trust you, Nicola."

Papa scribbled a note and put it in my hand. "I want you to give this to the bus driver. I want you to apologize to that girl, you hear?"

Papa hated disorderly conduct. He thought everything would be all right once I said I was sorry.

The next afternoon, I came home with a note from the bus driver.

Papa dropped the note and bent down to my face. "I'm ashamed of what you did, Nicola. Why didn't you tell her you were sorry?"

"I didn't do anything wrong! I didn't push her."

"Enough!" He grabbed me by the shoulder. "Say you're sorry and go up to your room."

"I won't say it."

"Go to the basement and stay down there until you do."

I went to the basement and shut the door. Papa made himself a sandwich and brewed a fresh pot of coffee. It was getting dark. After eating the sandwich Papa came down to the basement. I sat in the dark, cradling my head between my drawn-up knees.

"Stand up!" he said.

I tried, but my legs gave way under me. Papa grabbed me by the collar, yanked me up. "Have you come to your senses?"

I didn't answer him.

"I want to hear it."

I stood, tucking my chin against my chest.

"You know why you're down here, so let's hear it."

In a small voice I said, "I think I wet my pants."

Papa felt the seat of my pants. "Say you're sorry, then go up and change."

"I can't say I'm sorry. I didn't do it."

I sat back down, covering my head with my hands.

"Go upstairs! Wash up!"

I went upstairs, washed, and ate dinner. That night in my sleep I saw Papa standing in the doorway like a blanched photograph. I cried, "Papa, I didn't do anything wrong!" When I woke I heard the piano downstairs.

I climbed out of bed, padded barefoot downstairs, and stood quietly at the foot of the stairs. A night-light as dim and soft as a low-burning candle lit the living room. At the piano, you were singing, *Go to sleep, baby child, Hush-a-bye, don't you cry. When you wake, you shall have, All the pretty little horses*. When you stopped, I went to you. Half turned, you saw me and pulled me to your bosom.

"What happened, baby?" you asked hoarsely.

"Nothing," I said, pressing my cheek against your warm chest.

"Did Mama wake you?"

"Why don't you go to bed?"

"I'm not sleepy, hon."

You kissed me on the cheek, and on your breath I smelled the sweet odor of brandy. I put my arms around you and closed my eyes. I felt not sleepy but dreamy in your softness and warmth.

"Can I sleep with you?"

"I go to bed very late, hon."

"I'll wait for you."

"You know you have to get up for school early in the morning, don't you?"

I peeked at you with one eye. "You won't wake me up when you come in. Papa never wakes me up. So can I?"

"I'm used to sleeping alone, hon." Then you looked down at me and gently laid my head in your lap. "I need a drink or two," you said, "before I go to bed. That helps me sleep."

"Will you ever be cured?"

"Listen, it's late. Go on back to bed." Then you glided your fingers across the keyboard. The sound rippled merrily.

"Can I stay here with you?"

You knitted your brows. "What for?"

"I just want to be with you."

"I don't want you to be tired in the morning."

You lifted my head from your lap, and I knew I shouldn't insist. You'd get upset.

I went back to my bed and soon I slept to the sound of the piano. Mama, I saw Chi Lan in a white dress sitting by a canal in the Plain of Reeds. She was as cute as a hamster. I know she could only speak English and not many words in Vietnamese since you adopted her as a child. But I heard her voice, Mama. Her voice was Vietnamese. She has serene eyes, elongated and pretty. This orphan child, having been displaced to grow up into a beautiful girl, who exudes liveliness and consideration. *Why a Vietnamese adopted child?* Did this somehow allow you to hold on to the memory of me, your lost son?

When I woke in the dark, I sat up, looking at the blurred white of the bedroom door, beyond it the hallway and your bedroom. As quietly as I could, I gathered my pillow in my arms and crawled out of bed. The floor creaked as I tiptoed from the room. The smell of brandy hung in the air. Light from the front porch gleamed on the white curtains. The breeze carried in the earth-dry smell of grass. Afraid to wake you, I lay down at the foot of the bed next to your feet under the bedcover. I watched the curtains rise and fall in the breeze, listened to the dry sounds of autumn leaves on the lawn, and no longer feeling the tugging at my heart, I slept.

╬

AUTHOR BIO

Khanh Ha is the author of *Flesh and The Demon Who Peddled Longing*. He is a seven-time Pushcart nominee, finalist for the Mary McCarthy Prize, Many Voices Project, Prairie Schooner Book Prize, and The University of New Orleans Press Lab Prize. He is the recipient of the Sand Hills Prize for Best Fiction, the Robert Watson Literary Prize in Fiction, The Orison Anthology Award for Fiction, and The C&R Press Fiction Prize. His new novel, *Mrs. Rossi's Dream*, was named Best New Book by Booklist.

C&R PRESS TITLES

NONFICTION

By the Bridge or By the River by Amy Roma
Women in the Literary Landscape by Doris Weatherford, et al
Credo: An Anthology of Manifestos & Sourcebook for Creative Writing by Rita Banerjee and Diana Norma Szokolyai

FICTION

Last Tower to Heaven by Jacob Paul
History of the Cat in Nine Chapters or Less by Anis Shivani
No Good, Very Bad Asian by Lelund Cheuk
Surrendering Appomattox by Jacob M. Appel
Made by Mary by Laura Catherine Brown
Ivy vs. Dogg by Brian Leung
While You Were Gone by Sybil Baker
Cloud Diary by Steve Mitchell
Spectrum by Martin Ott
That Man in Our Lives by Xu Xi

SHORT FICTION

A Mother's Tale & Other Stories by Khanh Ha
Fathers of Cambodian Time-Travel Science by Bradley Bazzle
Two Californias by Robert Glick
Notes From the Mother Tongue by An Tran
The Protester Has Been Released by Janet Sarbanes

ESSAY AND CREATIVE NONFICTION

Selling the Farm by Debra Di Blasi
the internet is for real by Chris Campanioni
Immigration Essays by Sybil Baker
Death of Art by Chris Campanioni

POETRY

How to Kill Yourself Instead of Your Children by Qunicy S. Jones
Lottery of Intimacies by Jonathan Katz
What Feels Like Love by Tom C. Hunley
The Rented Altar by Lauren Berry
Between the Earth and Sky by Eleanor Kedney
What Need Have We for Such as We by Amanda Auerbach
A Family Is a House by Dustin Pearson
The Miracles by Amy Lemmon
Banjo's Inside Coyote by Kelli Allen
Objects in Motion by Jonathan Katz
My Stunt Double by Travis Denton
Lessons in Camoflauge by Martin Ott
Millennial Roost by Dustin Pearson
All My Heroes are Broke by Ariel Francisco
Holdfast by Christian Anton Gerard
Ex Domestica by E.G. Cunningham
Like Lesser Gods by Bruce McEver
Notes from the Negro Side of the Moon by Earl Braggs
Imagine Not Drowning by Kelli Allen
Notes to the Beloved by Michelle Bitting
Free Boat: Collected Lies and Love Poems by John Reed
Les Fauves by Barbara Crooker
Tall as You are Tall Between Them by Annie Christain
The Couple Who Fell to Earth by Michelle Bitting
Notes to the Beloved by Michelle Bitting

CPSIA information can be obtained
at www.ICGtesting.com
Printed in the USA
BVHW050739291021
620153BV00006B/113